The Hand
in the
Window

I0628114

Elizabeth Young

DIVERTIR
PUBLISHING
Salem, NH

The Hand in the Window

Elizabeth Young

Copyright © 2018 Elizabeth Young

Cover design by Kenneth Tupper

Published by Divertir Publishing LLC
PO Box 232
North Salem, NH 03073
http://www.divertirpublishing.com/

ISBN-13: 978-1-938888-24-3
ISBN-10: 1-938888-24-3

Library of Congress Control Number: 2018966257

Printed in the United States of America

This story was written, in part, to honor the tireless road crews who work throughout our country. Their service all too often goes unnoticed. And, as always, I dedicate the book to my husband and best critic.

Contents

PROLOGUE

GETTING THE KID into the car proved easy. Getting him out at the other end where he was going to be hidden involved chloroform, and too much of that could kill the youngster. They didn't want him dead—the kid would be returned when the money was paid. That part shouldn't take too long, or so his partner assured him.

Everything went according to plan that night. When it was over, he felt relieved. After all, this wasn't a real kidnapping. They were just borrowing the kid to settle a debt, of sorts. He turned off the flashlight and left in the dark.

CHAPTER ONE

"RUN, RUN!" the big man next to Jay screamed at the skinny boy heading toward third base. Jay moved a couple of inches away from the man and closer to his wife, Emma, who stayed where she was.

"Good play, Tim," Jay called out to his own son, playing third base, when he tagged out the runner, much to the vocal disgust of the kid's father—or whoever he was. Tim couldn't hear Jay, but Jay would be sure to compliment him later.

One more out and the game would be over, the ten-year-old boys exhausted but pumped, and all of them hungry. Tim's team was about to win by six runs, one of which had been Tim's solo home run in the second inning. "I think you make a great third baseman," Jay told Tim earlier in the summer, which was his way of saying he didn't mind that Tim wasn't pitching, something he himself had done at Tim's age. "You have great hands, great coordination, and you're fast!"

They talked about baseball a lot, and now that Tim was older, he understood and liked the strategy of the game. Sometimes Jay wondered if, without baseball, the separation might have made Tim mad at him, but Tim never talked about it. He seemed a little sad sometimes, especially when Jay would spend an evening at the house, have dinner with the three of them, and then leave to go back to where he was living temporarily—in Alex Rosen's garage apartment. At first he had worried more about how six-year-old Lynn would take it, but she always seemed cheerful when he told her he would be back soon. And, of course, he always came back.

"Come on," he said when the last boy on the Tigers flied out. He held out his hands to Lynn and pulled her up. "Your brother will meet us at the car, and then we're all going out for pizza!"

Lynn wrinkled her nose just a little, reminding Jay of her mother's similar habit when she was annoyed. "Can't I have a chicken sandwich?" the little girl asked, looking from Jay to Emma. Her mother laughed. "Of course you can! We'll go to Dano's, and you can have whatever you like, but your brother will want pizza."

They climbed down from the bleachers and headed over to the van, which, Jay knew, would be hot. Even when it was running, the air conditioning barely worked. That was one of the reasons he had given his truck to Emma to drive when they separated three months ago. He would drive her van and try to keep it running. Now, in mid-August, he missed the reliability of his Ford 150.

"Dad, I really like the glove—thank you!" Tim gave his father a hug at the door of the van, which Jay started to get the air conditioning going.

"Well, you know how to use it—that last inning was terrific. And so was your homer. Guess I'll have to get you a new bat next," Jay said, returning the hug.

Lynn leaned out the window in the back where she and Emma were waiting. "Good game, Timmy," she yelled enthusiastically. "Get in—Dad's going to take us to Dano's to *eat*!"

During the short drive, both kids talked at once, while Emma said nothing. Jay stole a glance at her a couple of times in the rearview mirror. She seemed all right, but he wished he knew how she was feeling. More than that, he wished he knew if she was still seeing Patrick McNaughton from work. They hadn't separated because of Patrick; he came along later, or so Jay thought. What she said at the time was that she was tired of Jay's working all the time and basically ignoring her and that she "didn't want to live like this anymore." Try as he might, Jay had not yet been able to figure out exactly what that meant. He always tried to be there for important events, and especially for the children, attending school plays, PTA meetings, sports events, and even church events, although he didn't attend church very often.

"We'll have two medium pizzas, one 'supreme' and one with just pepperoni and cheese," Jay told the waitress, who had already brought them water and a lemonade for Lynn. "And one chicken sandwich on toasted white bread with lots of mayonnaise."

"I'd like a 7-Up, too," Tim added politely, and the waitress smiled at him. With his auburn cowlick and mannerly ways, he usually appealed to adults. People said he looked like his father, but Jay, who was fair with curly black hair, didn't see it.

Conversation during the meal progressed from details of the game to the outlook for the team to get into the citywide playoffs in three weeks. Finally, Emma looked directly at Jay and asked, "Where are you working next week?"

"Same road," Jay said, carefully folding his paper napkin and laying it on the table. "I'm still holding one of the signs. They ran into a problem digging the ditch for the water pipe, so we'll probably be there three or four more weeks. They're trenching, laying, and doing a temporary paving. But no weekend work. I told Alex I'd help him with the orchard, but just for a few hours, so I can help you and the kids most of next weekend."

"Will you come to my game Saturday, Dad?" Tim asked with a mouthful of pizza.

"Don't talk with your mouth full!" Jay answered automatically, and then ruffled his son's hair. "You know I will, and if you get rained out, we'll find something else to do." He saw Emma smile faintly. After he paid for the meal, they piled back into the van and he drove them to the house. *But not my home anymore*, he thought. He wondered if it ever would be again. The children had stopped asking if he would spend the night. He wondered what Emma told them. A couple of weeks ago, when he and Tim were together at Walmart, Tim asked, "Dad, are you ever going to move back in?"

"Your mother and I have some things to work out, Tim, and we're trying to do that. We both love you and Lynn very much. I'll let you know anything we decide once we decide it." Tim had not asked the question since.

After he went in with them, read Lynn a story, examined Tim's ant farm, and went over some bills with Emma, Jay left. It was early, but he didn't feel like going to the Brick Bat for a beer. He drove back to his garage apartment, popped a cold Heineken, and turned on a tennis match. He didn't really care about the match, but his choices were limited with no cable hookup. Tomorrow he was going to work in the orchard with Alex Rosen, his landlord, which he didn't mind. It was good physical work and much more interesting than holding the "stop/go" sign on a country road for eight hours. He reminded himself, however, for all the boredom of that job, the pay was good.

CHAPTER TWO

THE PROBLEM NEARLY every morning that Jay got up to go to work was that he had to dress in layers. Even in August, it could be very cool in the mornings at their elevation, which meant at least a jacket and a sweater over his tee shirt. This Monday morning he added a loose-fitting, long-sleeved cotton shirt over the tee. After gulping his coffee and filling his thermos with what remained of the pot, he added all the top layers of clothes and walked out to the van, which started after the third try. He figured that in two more weeks he would have enough cash to take it into the shop for repairs again. He began his ten-mile drive to the work site.

When he got there, two trucks were already parked in the workers' temporary lot, which was really just an open, rutted field. Jay recognized Tyrone's old blue Chevy Tahoe and Carlos' late-model Toyota Tundra, which was a model Jay had his eye on—if he could ever afford a new truck. Carlos, as foreman, almost always got to the job site first. Today he was up in the cab of the front loader, getting it started so he could move it into place for the driver, who always seemed to be late. Jay admired Carlos, who was fair, a hard worker, and skilled—he could run most of the equipment if somebody called in sick or didn't show up.

Jay pulled out his thermos, a large bottle of water, his lunch bag with the usual bologna and cheese sandwich, and an apple. He dumped them all into a white plastic bag and began walking to the equipment shed. By the time he retrieved his sign and walkie-talkie from the locker, greeted Carlos, and walked to his post, he already felt warm. He shrugged off his jacket and saw Tyrone had arrived. Tyrone would be holding the sign at the other end of the construction zone. They used the walkie-talkies to keep in touch, which was necessary as they were working along a curve in the road and could not see each other.

They began stopping the traffic at 8 a.m. and worked until 4 p.m., taking staggered lunch breaks, with one of the other crew relieving them for half an hour. Jay's break would come at noon, with Tyrone getting off at 12:30. If they didn't want to eat in their vehicles, there were some tall pine trees just off to one side of the road, with a sloping bank and soft grass under them. It made a good shady spot for lunch, although Jay sometimes had trouble staying awake. That's when he usually drank the rest of the coffee in the thermos.

Two of the pipe layers were rolling the "CAUTION—ONE LANE" signs into place on both ends of the construction zone. Jay was already beginning to feel bored. The pay was better than what he had been making at the factory, though, and the job gave him health benefits that covered the family. He hadn't made any close friends on the crew, as this was the first job working with them. He liked several of them well enough, and they exchanged easy pleasantries. Plus, the job gave him time to think. Besides baseball and the van, Jay tried to think about the family and what to do next. Except that as many ideas as he had, they all took more money than he had.

He often considered moving to North Carolina. His mother and step-father lived there and had a growing nursery business. He had studied agricultural business during his two years at Tech, before he dropped out because of the money. He liked working with plants and knew he was good at it. When he lost the job at the factory, his parents invited him to join them. At the time, he thought Emma wouldn't like that, although he never asked her. His real fantasy involved taking just Tim with him and starting a new life, but then he felt guilty about Lynn and Emma, too.

"Okay, the red Volks with Ohio tags is my last one," Tyrone's voice crackled through the walkie-talkie. Jay waited for the small red car. Then he slowly turned his sign from "stop" to "proceed with caution." The first car in his stopped line eased out; a blond woman was driving, and she smiled at him. Most people never looked at him, and some frowned, as if he, personally, was keeping them in the waiting line. Once in a while someone smiled and waved. Jay let his twenty cars go through before turning his sign back to "stop" and calling Tyrone to let him know that a white Toyota Highlander was his last car.

By the time Jay finished his lunch break under the pine trees, he had shed his sweater as well as his jacket. Since he didn't want to bother walking back to his van, he bundled them up and put them in the plastic bag by the side of the road near him. The traffic in the afternoon was always sparse. No cars came by in either direction for twenty minutes, and by three o'clock Jay was fighting drowsiness. He drained the thermos and began looking around, trying to get interested in something other than the pavement and the four men in white hard hats laying the water pipe.

Across the road he noticed tall corn was growing. He wasn't sure if the corn was for cattle or people. On his side of the road, but well back from it, was a one-story, ranch-style red brick house. The sign halfway up the long drive said "for sale." Jay had noticed the sign the first time he looked at the house, but today he realized that there was no realtor's name—just a phone number.

A car was coming. He made sure his sign was turned to "stop." As he watched to see if more cars were coming, he realized he had never seen anyone near the brick house. He wondered if it was occupied or if the owners had moved out. He did not remember seeing any cars pulling into the driveway. To the right of the house stood scraggly woods made up of some bushes, jack pines, and oaks. The nearest structures to the left of the house were a farmer's shed and a white farmhouse. They were at least fifty yards down the road and even further back from it than the brick house. *Guess you don't see your neighbors very much out here,* Jay thought, turning his sign to let his two cars through after calling Tyrone. They usually waited for twenty cars to get in line before letting the line go, but when there was so little traffic they just used common sense.

Another lull in the traffic. To distract himself, Jay turned toward the brick house. It had a garage on the far right side. The main part of the house to the left of the garage jutted out, with a recessed front door in the middle and three windows about five feet off the ground to the left of the door. Just then his walkie-talkie crackled. "Got three comin' through—last one's a big brown Dodge van." Jay started to turn back toward the traffic that would be coming at him, but his gaze lingered for a second on the front of the house.

Then he saw it. The sight lasted no more than a couple of seconds, but in the window furthest to his left, he saw what he was sure was a hand. A small one, maybe a child's, maybe a woman's, but a hand—the palm facing towards him, the fingers and thumb splayed out. And then it was gone.

Jay spun around to get his sign turned. The first car from Tyrone's end was approaching. Jay felt his heart beating, his adrenalin pumping. Now thoroughly awake, he held his sign steady and concentrated on the traffic. Cars began queuing up on his side, too. Less than an hour to go and traffic was picking up. What rush hour there was started about 4:30 p.m., which was why they quit at 4:00. The men digging today had made some progress, but not much. Several times in the last three weeks they

9

experienced the ditch collapsing, and Jay saw that happen again today. Now he hoped he wouldn't have to move down the road at least for another day or two. He wanted that much time to see if he could see anything going on at the brick house. In one way, he hoped he had just been sleepy and confused. Could he have just seen a piece of paper flapping in the window? In another way, he wanted to see the hand again.

CHAPTER THREE

TUESDAY BROUGHT NO unusual events on the job. The day dawned warm, and Jay wore fewer clothes. The van behaved. He treated himself to lukewarm fried chicken for lunch, picking it up at a KFC on his way to work. He brought two Cokes and plenty of water. He spent as much time as he could looking at the house, but he saw nothing, and no one came or went. There was no way to tell if it was occupied. During his lunch break, he casually asked two of the other workers if they knew anything about the house, but they didn't. "Why, you thinking of buying it?" one of them asked him, raising an eyebrow. Most of them knew he had been laid off at the factory and that he was glad to have this job; none of them knew he was separated from his wife.

When he turned in his sign and walkie-talkie at the end of his shift, Carlos was locking up equipment. "We will have a new person with us tomorrow," he informed Jay in his slightly formal English. Carlos' family came from Florida, by way of Cuba. "And she is a lady. I will ask you to give her an orientation to your position at some point. She will be working to relieve you and Tyrone and also running one of the tillers."

Jay nodded. He didn't think there was much training required to show anyone what he did, but he was curious about the new worker.

On Wednesday, Jay showed up at the work site even earlier than his usual time. Only one other car, a Hyundai Elantra, had already arrived. Jay hoped that maybe he would see a car parked in the driveway or leaving the brick house, but he didn't. When Carlos arrived in his Tundra, Jay got out of the van and went to collect his sign and walkie-talkie.

"Jay, I would like you to meet Rebecca Franz. She is now part of our crew." Carlos smiled at both of them as a woman who looked to be in her mid-twenties got out of the Hyundai.

"It's Becky," she said in a low, pleasant voice, smiling at Jay.

"Jay Berg here," he said, giving her a small smile.

"I will put her with you first today," Carlos explained. Becky was carrying a dark blue satchel that Jay thought probably contained her lunch and whatever else she had brought. He felt disappointed that he wouldn't have time to do any surveillance of the house right away on his shift, but then he admitted to himself that training Becky might be interesting, and there probably wouldn't be anything to see at the house anyway.

"We wait for twenty cars to line up, and then we talk to each other and confirm what's happening at the other end. For example, Tyrone will tell me the make and model of the last car in his line, so I know when his line ends. I wait about five seconds and then turn my sign. We don't get all that much traffic out here. Just sometimes in the late afternoon. Carlos keeps the key to the locker in the shed, so if you need batteries for the walkie-talkie or anything, that's where to get them." Jay paused, feeling a little awkward now. "And if you need a rest break or anything, switch your walkie-talkie to Carlos' frequency and ask him to send a man to relieve you."

Becky smiled. "Sounds easy enough. How long have you been on the job?"

"It's my fourth week. Mainly been holding the sign, but Carlos said he may use me for some of the trenching work later. Looks like the work on this road is going to last through September. You going to work with us full time?"

"For now. I'm going to school at the community college nights, starting in September. I need the money, and I'm hoping I can juggle the schedule so I can work here during the day."

Jay looked at his watch. Five minutes to start time. "Do you want to take the sign for the first run?" He turned on the walkie-talkie. He had seen Tyrone arrive about ten minutes ago. "Ty, we're ready here—Becky's taking the first run." Jay assumed Carlos had told Tyrone about Becky.

"All ready here," Tyrone radioed back, and Jay handed the walkie-talkie to Becky.

Thirty minutes later, Becky radioed Tyrone that she'd like to come down and work with him. He agreed, so she turned back the equipment to Jay. "Good going," Jay said, smiling, and Becky returned his smile. She picked up her satchel from the side of the road and began walking away from Jay. Jay observed that she was shorter than Emma, who was nearly as tall as Jay, and Becky certainly had more curves. Jay liked his women lean and admired long legs, but he found Becky walking away very sexy even in old blue jeans and a work shirt. Her short, black hair looked like a cap over her head, covering her small ears. Emma seldom wore jeans and always dressed up a little bit, even to work. Sometimes, when Jay asked her to, she also wore perfume, which he liked.

By midafternoon, storm clouds were gathering west of the work site. "Gonna quit early," Tyrone radioed to Jay. "Carlos jus' came over to tell me and said for me to tell you. Hafta wait for the work crew to move their stuff, then we can cut off. Should be 'bout three o'clock." Jay suddenly felt let down. Not that the work stimulated him that much, but nothing had happened at the brick house, and he hadn't seen Becky more than in the distance since the morning. She was working with the tiller in the middle of the day, and Tyrone spelled Jay off at lunch while Becky stood in for Tyrone.

Fifteen minutes later, they heard the first rumbles of thunder. Fortunately, the two men assigned to the closing-down tasks were folding up the "Caution—One Lane" signs, after which Jay and Tyrone could quit. Within ten minutes, splashes of rain started, and by then, all of the crew were sprinting toward their vehicles. Jay got to the shed last and handed in his equipment. "Becky did fine with us," he told Carlos, who smiled as he locked up.

"Check the web site in the morning to see if we work," he reminded Jay. "No rain is predicted, so I think we will." Jay nodded and hoped Carlos was right. They didn't get paid for days off because of bad weather.

Jay got into his van very slowly and pretended to be stowing his bag. He wanted to be the last one to leave the parking field. He turned the van north on the road and drove back to where he had been standing all day. Two trucks were headed toward him, going in the opposite direction. There was no one behind him when he drew abreast of the house. He had already decided what he would do. He turned into the driveway, turned off the ignition, and slouched down in his seat. If anyone came or challenged him, he would say he was thinking about buying the house. But no one came. The rain poured down heavily, but Jay could see blue sky beyond the overhanging cloud.

After twenty minutes, Jay was ready to give it up. The rain had stopped, leaving the air cooler, so he lowered a window, but the van still felt stuffy. No sign of life at the house. Jay started the engine. He could back out or turn around in the driveway. He decided to turn around.

He gave the house one more glance, especially the high windows on the left—and he saw it again: the hand at the window. This time, it seemed smaller. Then Jay realized that the fingers were curling inward, as if someone was clawing at the glass. In his mind, he heard a scream. The fingers moved for a few seconds, and then the hand disappeared.

Jay cut off the engine and simply sat, staring at the house. His heart was racing. "I should do something," he said out loud, but he couldn't imagine what. What if someone was in there, maybe a child, in trouble? He gripped the steering wheel hard. "Maybe I should tell someone," he said, hardly hearing his own voice. And who would that be? The deputy sheriff, his brother-in-law, who had told Jay to his face that he thought Jay was an alcoholic, just because Jay had been hitting the beer pretty heavily for a time after the separation. He couldn't imagine convincing Vic that he was stone cold sober while seeing a mysterious hand at the window of an apparently vacant house.

He thought about telling Carlos but rejected the idea because Carlos might of heard that Jay used to drink—and Carlos had the power to fire Jay.

As he looked again at the house, he knew the windows were too high for him to see directly in. He would need a ladder to do that. Then he had another idea. *What if I'm not imagining this and someone's in there, someone in trouble? Maybe I can look in the newspaper or go online and see if there's been any kind of a kidnapping or a missing person report.* The Telegraph served as a weekly county newspaper, and while it carried lots of ads, it did report on community and state news. Jay had only a vague idea about how to use the Internet to check on missing persons in the area, but he knew he could try.

He sat in the driveway another twenty minutes, but nothing appeared again at any of the windows. So he started the van and headed for his house. He hadn't said he would be over for dinner that night, but Emma always seemed to cook extra, and he knew that Tim and Lynn would be happy to see him. At least he hoped so.

CHAPTER FOUR

D AD, COME AND see my charts!" Tim had taken Jay's hand after dinner and practically dragged his father from the kitchen table. When they got to Tim's room, Jay saw his son had used the computer to make elaborate charts of which American League teams were winning, who they would play for the rest of the season, and who might survive to the playoffs and the World Series. The Boston Red Socks figured prominently in Tim's hopeful calculations.

"They're really good, Tim," Jay said with honest admiration. In school, Tim excelled at math, a talent Jay hoped had come from him.

"Dad, if the Sox win the pennant, will you take me to the World Series?"

Jay laughed. Tim had asked him this question every year. Jay put a sober look on his face and said in a solemn voice, "We'll see." His son groaned, knowing that the answer probably meant "no," but he half hoped that this year it would be different.

Before leaving the room, Jay glanced at Tim's computer and saw a page about Morse code up on the screen. A printed copy lay in the printer tray.

"Are you studying that?" Jay asked.

Tim nodded. "For my scouting badge. My scoutmaster says it's good to know. He says people use computers and things too much, and we need to know how get along without them."

Jay nodded. "Morse used to be what people on ships used. I had a friend when I was your age, and we studied Morse, too. Is it hard for you to learn?"

"Nah—I memorized everything pretty much right away."

Jay realized some time ago his son probably had close to a photographic memory. And he liked to read, which made Jay feel good—he and Emma gave both children books for presents even when they were very young.

"I'm going to read your sister a story, and then let's toss some balls outside before it gets dark," Jay said, ruffling Tim's hair.

Emma had cleaned the kitchen and was sitting in the living room, reading a book. She smiled when Jay came into the room. He smiled back. "Is it okay if I put Lynn to bed and read her a story?"

"Sure, she'd like that. She's into the 'Chronicles of Narnia' right now—it's on the table by her bed."

Jay found Lynn sitting on the front porch, intently watching a caterpillar that was crawling very slowly down the steps. He sat down with her. "Do you think that caterpillar will turn into a butterfly?" he asked seriously.

"Yep. But first it turns into a cris-liss!"

"You mean a chrysalis," Jay said, smiling.

"Whatever!"

"How about I read to you from your book and tuck you in tonight? It's about your bedtime."

Instead of arguing, Lynn got up, took his hand, and led him back into the house.

Nice family picture, Jay said to himself with a twinge as they walked by Emma, who looked up from her book. *Wish it was true.* He thought about asking Emma how things were at work—meaning, of course, whether she was still seeing Patrick—but then he felt that he couldn't really deal with all that tonight.

Earlier, when he was driving to the house, he remembered his and Emma's first date—at a ball game. Jay had loved the way Emma wore her long hair up, the smooth skin on her arms and hands, and her scent. Two more dates and a long weekend together in the mountains and he was ready to propose. They were happy together those first few years. They made love most nights, and when Tim came everything seemed perfect. Where did it all go?

When he came back into the living room after reading two chapters to a sleepy Lynn and tucking her in, he said, "Tim and I are going out to play catch for a while before I go."

"Mmmm," she said, not looking up. Jay went outside where Tim was already warming up his throwing arm by aiming the baseball against a large oak. Half an hour later, with most of the light gone from the sky, Jay said, "That's it for tonight, Tim. I'll be at your game Saturday if I don't get back here before then." For just a second, Jay saw Tim's mouth droop, but then he smiled at his father and simply said, "Okay—thanks for working with me on my throwing. Coach says I'm getting better. He might even let me pitch next season!"

After returning briefly to the living room to say goodbye to Emma, who did not get up, Jay got into the van and realized he did not want to go back to his apartment. Going out for a drink didn't appeal to him either, so he found himself heading back to the job site. It was past nine o'clock. He didn't know what he expected to see, but he knew that what he was going to do was to watch the brick house for a while.

Jay rolled the windows of the van down so he wouldn't have to run the air conditioning, which put a load on the old battery. He was approaching the house from the south. Suddenly he saw a car coming toward him with no lights on. He slowed down. The car got to the driveway of the house and turned in. Jay could make out that it was a sedan, but he couldn't see much else and certainly not the license plate. With his own lights still on, he drove past the driveway and continued for half a mile, looking for a good place to turn around and double back. When he got to a turn off on the road, he reversed his direction and drove back. This time, when he was almost abreast of the driveway, he came to a stop. The car he had seen was at the end of the driveway, near the front door of the house. No lights from the car and none from the house.

Jay wished he had binoculars. He didn't know how long he could just stay stopped on the road before some other cars came, but he half hoped the person who drove the sedan would come back, get in, and drive down the driveway so at least Jay could see something more about the car. When, after ten minutes, that didn't happen, Jay slowly accelerated and headed for home. He drove carefully, but he was working on a plan. He also thought that if he could borrow some binoculars, he could watch the house after dark the next night.

But an hour later, back at his apartment, Jay felt frustrated. When he called the number on the "for sale" sign, he got a message "this number is no longer in service." Then he looked at a "multiple listings" web site to see if the house was listed for sale. No luck. He entered the address of the house into several web sites that promised to give owner information if you had the address, but he kept getting a "no listed owner" message. It certainly seemed to Jay that someone must own the house, as someone was trying to sell it. Jay felt frustrated enough to end his search. Then he thought of something else.

His brother-in-law, Vic, once showed him—and Tim—how to log on to crime sites. Tim found it fascinating. Jay hadn't paid much attention, but he remembered enough to do it now. When he got to the site for his county, he found plenty of listings of unsolved breaking and entering incidents, arrests, names of people wanted for parole violation and the like, but there were no kidnappings or missing persons listed for the last year.

17

Well, I guess I could camp out in the woods tomorrow night, Jay decided. That idea seemed a little foolish to him now, but he didn't have any other plan. He knew it would help if he had somebody he could talk to about all of this. He went over his short list of friends and wondered if Becky might be interested in the mystery. In his short time knowing her, she seemed smart. Maybe she would even have some suggestions.

Jay sat in the dark, with only the glow of his laptop screen illuminating the apartment and thought about the next day. He'd talk to Becky either before they started work—if she got there early—or during the lunch break. If she had a good idea about something else he could do, short of sitting in the woods in the van in the dark, he'd listen. Or maybe she'd like his idea and volunteer to come with him.

"Yeah, sure," Jay said out loud, getting up to turn on the TV for the late news. But he had to admit he was looking forward to going to work on Thursday.

CHAPTER FIVE

THURSDAY MORNING JAY arrived at the work site thirty minutes before his start time and felt gratified when Becky's Elantra pulled up right next to his van. He got out first and opened her door for her. She laughed at that and said, "Your mama must have brought you up right!" Jay didn't know what to say, so he launched right into what he been thinking about all night.

"If you have a minute after we check in, I want to ask you about something," he said, keeping his voice low.

Becky's eyebrows went up. "You sound serious. If you mean that, sure. I'll follow you down to your station. I think I'm going to be working with the rolling crew this morning, then spelling you at lunch, but I can come with you for a few minutes now."

They checked in. After Jay retrieved his walkie-talkie and sign they began walking down the road. "I know you're going to think I'm crazy, but I've seen something, and I don't know what to do about it." Becky stopped walking and turned to look at him.

"Come on, keep walking," Jay said, glancing behind him. Some of the men were starting up their machines, and the noise level on the road was picking up.

"There's this house, the red brick one with the 'for sale' sign that I've been standing in front of. Nobody ever seems to come or go there, but two days ago and then again yesterday when I was sort of looking at the house, I saw a hand in one of the windows." He paused to let this sink in.

"A *hand*? You mean like a real live human hand?" This time, Becky kept up their pace, but she turned her head to look at him again.

"Yeah, like somebody was below the window and holding up their hand. It looked small, like maybe a child's or a small woman's. Last night, after we quit, I drove back there, went up the driveway and waited almost half an hour. That's when I saw it the second time. I drove back here after dinner, too, and I saw a car drive in the driveway. I think it didn't have any license plates, but I couldn't tell for sure."

19

"You think it might just be something hanging above the window and it comes into view now and then?"

"I thought of that, but I couldn't see a string or rope or anything. And it's coming up at the bottom of the window. My eyesight's pretty good. It looked like a real hand."

Becky was silent for a moment. "Do you know anything about who owns the house? Can you go on line and find out?"

"Tried that, and no, I can't find out anything. There's a phone number on the 'for sale' sign, but it's not a working number. Nobody on the crew seems to know. I've asked some of them. I looked at the house sale listings online and it's not listed, and none of the web sites I checked show an owner's name. Kinda strange if it's really for sale."

They were almost at his station, and start time was ten minutes away. Becky paused. "I have a friend who sells real estate part time. She could probably find out who owns it."

"I'm going back there tonight," Jay blurted out. He hadn't planned on revealing this right away, but it just came out. "I'm going to borrow some binoculars and park the van in the woods and wait to see if the car comes back—or if I can see anything else."

"I could text my friend and then call her when I'm on break," Becky said, and he was relieved to see that she was not laughing at him. "If she can find out something, maybe you wouldn't have to camp out in the woods." Now he did hear a little humor in her voice. "I'll let you know what she says." She paused. Then, looking right at him, "Have you thought about going to the sheriff's office?"

Jay didn't feel like explaining his relationship with his brother-in-law, so he simply said, "Yeah, but I'd feel foolish if this was all some kind of a trick or something that I am just imagining. So I feel like I should have some more information first."

"Sounds reasonable. I'll get back to you." Becky shifted her work bag to her other hand and headed back down the road to where she would be joining the crew who did rolling to smooth the ditches before the pipe was laid. Jay envied her the physical labor, but for once he didn't mind standing with his sign. At least it gave him the opportunity to observe the house, which in the morning light looked no different than it had the day before—no car in the driveway, and nothing to be seen at the windows.

Four hours later, Becky arrived back at Jay's station. "I'm your lunch replacement," she said cheerfully. Then, looking around to see if anyone else was in earshot, she added, "Got a text message back from my real estate friend. She says the listed owner of the house is the estate of Carver Billingsley. Taxes are current. She didn't tell me anything else. Anything else you need?"

"Well, that helps. I can look up Carver Billingsley later. At least it's something."

Jay handed her the sign and walkie-talkie. He wanted to get out of the sun and had a shady spot under a pine picked out where he could eat his sandwich. "Thanks. I appreciate your checking." He almost added that maybe the whole thing was nothing, but he really didn't feel that way, and he didn't want to pretend with her. He walked over to the side of the road to pick up his bag.

"I wouldn't mind going with you tonight," Becky called to him as he started off to his lunch spot.

Jay stopped, turned around, and realized that this was exactly what he hoped she would say. "Well, that's fine, but let's talk about it when I come back. I'll be back in twenty minutes." And for once, he didn't mind taking a shorter lunch break.

CHAPTER SIX

JAY TOLD BECKY he would pick her up at just before dark, then drive back to the house, and find a place in the woods to park the van. "We should get there just before it's really dark," Jay told her. "And it might be a long wait, but if it's all right with you, I plan to stay until midnight." She agreed and offered to bring water and some cheese crackers.

Now it was dusk, and Jay was driving the van along a rutted path that led into the woods close enough to the house so they could watch it with Alex Rosen's night vision binoculars. Alex didn't ask why Jay wanted to borrow them but simply said, "Don't lose them!" when Jay picked them up after dinner.

"Hope this isn't going to be too long a night for you," Jay said to Becky as he was maneuvering the van into a tight spot between two stands of pines. He felt a little awkward with her now since this wasn't a work occasion, but it certainly wasn't a social one either.

"I took a nap when I got home earlier. And I had my call with Ben, so I'm fine."

"Who's Ben?"

"My fiancé. He's stationed at Fort Hood right now. Maybe going to Germany, but he doesn't know for sure. We talk most nights and text a lot." She paused. "I didn't exactly tell him about this little assignment. He's kinda jealous and has a temper sometimes."

Jay was at a loss for words, so he changed the subject. "How good is your eyesight? Can you see the house clearly from here?"

He parked the van facing the left side of the house about seventy-five yards away. Jay figured that they were reasonably well-concealed by the trees and small bushes. The almost-full moon shone brightly, and there would be a full sky of stars later.

"I can see it fine. I don't think we'll need the glasses until the car comes and we're trying to see who's in it or get the license number or something," Becky answered.

"Let's keep the windows down as long as we can—unless we get bugs," Jay suggested, pressing the buttons to lower the van's side windows. Becky nodded. Then Jay turned off the engine. For a while, neither of them spoke, and they could begin to hear the night noises—crickets, frogs, and the occasional rustling of grass and leaves from the passage of some small animal. Jay wondered if deer foraged here at night. If they saw the van, they would probably shy away. After thirty minutes when they had seen nothing unusual, Jay said to Becky, "Where you from originally? I can't place your accent."

She laughed softly. "Don't think I have one. I'm an Army brat. Both of my parents served. I was born in Kansas, moved to California, then Tennessee, then South Carolina. That's where my mom and dad are now. He's running a CarMax lot. I came here because of a boyfriend, but that ended and I stayed. Then I met Ben through a friend when he came to visit here. He used to live in Florida where his folks are—he still has a little place there, but he likes it here and we plan to settle down once he gets out of the service. By then, I want to have my college degree and get a real job." She arched her back and leaned as far back in the seat as she could to get more comfortable. That gave Jay a good look at her full breasts, which were stretching against the white cotton tee shirt that she had tucked into her khakis. "How about you?"

Jay sighed. He didn't want to get into his personal life with her, but he felt she deserved some kind of response. "Born and raised in the state but not in this county. Dad died when I was eight; Mom remarried. They live in North Carolina now, running a nursery. I started to study agriculture business at Tech, but the money ran out. I came here because of a job at the factory; my wife found a job there, too. Then they scaled back, and I was let go. That's when I got on the road crew. I have two kids—a boy and a girl."

"And your wife doesn't mind that you're sitting in the woods in the dark with another woman?" Jay could almost see Becky's eyebrows arching.

"We're separated. I live alone." He bit back the need to tell her more—to tell her that he didn't know what would happen next—a divorce, reconciliation, maybe just staying like this in limbo. That he hated Patrick McNaughton. That he wasn't even sure how he felt about Emma. That he loved his kids more than anything in the world.

"Sorry," Becky said softly, and then they were both quiet again. She opened a bottle of water and offered it to him.

A few minutes later they could see the stars, and the nearly full moon had risen high above them.

Within five minutes, a dark sedan approached the driveway to the house and turned in. Jay reached for the binoculars, which were under Becky's feet. She opened her bag and retrieved a small pad and pencil while he focused the binoculars. But their viewing angle was not good for seeing the license plates—if there were any. "Damn," Jay said very softly. And then the car swung ninety degrees in front of the house and stopped, and Jay could see the rear end quite well.

"He doesn't have any plates!" He handed Becky the glasses. She adjusted them slightly and held them up for a minute.

"He's got something in his hands, though," she said, quickly giving the binoculars back to Jay.

Jay readjusted them and looked. "Seems like a big sack or a garbage bag or something," he said, still look through the glasses. "He's got a key to the front door." The figure disappeared into the house. No lights came on, but they could both see a small pinprick of light that seemed to be moving around. "He must have a flashlight," Jay added, although the binoculars didn't help him to identify anything more now.

"Do you want me to sneak over there while he's inside and get a better look at the car?" Becky asked.

Jay turned to look at her and realized she was serious. "No! We can't risk letting him know that he's being watched." Privately, he had the same idea but didn't want either of them to get in trouble. "You know, he could just be the owner, and he comes at night because he works during the day. Maybe there's nothing strange about any of this. We have to be careful."

The pinprick of light entered the room with the window where Jay had seen the hand. Then it seemed to go out or at least become invisible. They waited. Jay adjusted the binoculars again but couldn't see anything more than the front of the house.

About half an hour later, the light reappeared in the window near the front door. Then it went out. The door opened. Still carrying a good-sized sack, the same figure emerged, turned, did something with the door—probably locking it—and got into the car. No headlights came on as the car slowly turned and drove down the driveway. Jay kept the binoculars up. "Looks like a late-model Chevy, probably black, but I can't be sure," he told Becky, who wrote this down.

"Do you want to follow him?" Becky asked before the car came to the main road.

"No, I don't want him to see us. And this damn van doesn't go very fast, so we'd probably lose him." They watched as the car came to the end of the driveway and turned to go in the direction away from where they were parked. They saw the tail lights come on a few seconds later, which meant he had finally turned on his headlights. Then the car was gone.

"Do you want to get into the house?" Becky asked.

"Not tonight," he said firmly, although he wanted to do that more than anything. "We need more information. Even if there's nothing going on in there, I want to find out a few things. Tell you what. After I take you home, I'll try to find out about this Carver Billingsley."

"Why don't you let me do the research? I'm pretty good with the on-line searches, and I can report back to you in the morning."

"Good idea. You're probably better at doing this online research than I am." Jay took one last look at the house with the binoculars. It was completely dark, and there were no signs of life.

He started the van's engine and carefully backed out of the small space. They drove to Becky's apartment in silence, but both of them were thinking. Jay briefly thought about asking her to join him at the Brick Bat for a beer, but he didn't feel like he wanted to turn this into a social occasion.

After he left her off, Jay checked his watch since the clock in the van had stopped working months ago. He decided to head to the Brick Bat. He needed time to think about what they'd seen and to decide what to do next, but he didn't want to go home to his small apartment and be by himself just yet. The Brick Bat would have news on the TV, too, or maybe a baseball game. He really missed cable.

CHAPTER SEVEN

ALL TWELVE TABLES at the Brick Bat were taken, so Jay moved to the bar and pulled out one of the high stools. Two men a couple of seats away were nursing beers and talking, while one gray-haired man sat alone at the end of the bar, drinking coffee. Jay ordered a Heineken. Both TV monitors were on, and he hoped to see some news and sports scores. One thing he liked about this bar was that they didn't play loud, inane music, and they would change the channels on the TV screens if you asked.

"And so I sent her a registered letter and told her that, if she didn't let me see Colley this weekend, I was going to call a lawyer." The younger of the two men near Jay reached for his glass.

His companion nodded. "Should scare her into it."

"Yeah, but I really can't afford it. So I hope it does. That bastard she's seeing probably thinks it's funny that she won't let me see my own kid."

Jay tried to tune out their conversation and concentrate on the sports scores. The Red Sox were having a good season and looked like World Series contenders, but so did the Minnesota Twins. They were playing each other tonight, in Minneapolis, and the score was tied at the bottom of the eighth. Other scores appeared on the crawler, and Jay watched them absently. He needed to decide how to get more information about the house and the mysterious car if he could. Plus, if there really was someone inside the house who needed help, he needed to do something soon.

The two men on his left had just ordered another round of beers. When they came, the older one said, "What's this new boyfriend of hers do, anyway? Is he maybe some kind of lawyer who's telling her how to get around your visitation rights?"

"Haven't any idea. I've never seen him real good—just that one time when he pulled up in his car when I was already in mine and going to leave. Colley ran into the house when he saw him, so I don't think Colley likes him, but Deb sure seems to. Says she's been seeing him for 'quite some time now'—whatever that means. Car looked kinda new. Maybe he deals drugs for all I know."

"So how long since you seen Colley?"

"Four weeks and counting."

Jay turned around to look directly at the two men. He moved over to the empty barstool next to them. "Mind if I horn in on your conversation?" For Jay, who seldom interrupted anybody and never insinuated himself into a group, this was completely out of character.

Both men turned to look at him, the older one frowning and the younger one raising an eyebrow. "It's a free world," he said listlessly.

"Thanks," Jay said, placing his beer bottle in front of him and signaling the bartender for another Heineken. "It's just that I couldn't help overhearing part of what you were saying," he said, nodded at the younger man, "and I'm going through a bad separation from my wife. Haven't gotten to the point of divorce yet, but it sounds like you have some experience—and I've got two kids I want to protect and keep seeing." The beer came and Jay took a long swallow. He hoped he had opened the conversational door.

Instantly, the younger man loosened his grip on his beer glass and gave Jay a half smile. "Sure, join the crowd. Name's Sid. This is my friend, Louie. I know *all* about divorce. Louie's been through it, too. But lately I'm thinking I did the whole thing wrong. Maybe should have stayed with her. Now my ex won't even let me see my son."

Jay merely nodded and said, "Bad scene, I guess." He took another swallow of his beer. "How old's your son?"

"Just turned six. Last time I saw him was at his birthday party. We took him to that party restaurant where they give the kids balloons and they make them into animals. He loved that."

Louie, who had been eyeing Jay curiously, broke in. "I think she wants more money from you, Sid. She knows about your dad dying and all. Has she asked for more?"

Sid stared at the bar. "Well, she did say something about I should be 'more generous' with her and Colley now that my old man had died, but I told her I was sticking with the alimony and support payments we agreed to in court. Fact is, he didn't leave me all that much, and they have to probate the estate first before I see any of it. I told her that." Sid looked up and glanced briefly at the TV monitor with the sports scores. "She mentioned it again but I still said 'no' and she got mad, but then she let it go."

Jay reached for the peanut bowl on the bar and pushed it toward Sid. "Does she work? Mine's at least got a good job. Makes more money than I do. Don't know what that would mean in a divorce."

Sid's mouth worked into a tight little smile. "She told the judge she only

28

works 'part-time' and that she volunteers a lot, but fact is she gets paid at the thrift shop where she volunteers, so she's got money, and they let her buy things dirt cheap. I'm regular with the alimony and support. She doesn't save though. She was always out buying stuff we didn't need."

"Who takes care of Colley during the day, I mean now that it's summer?" Jay asked, feeling that Sid's answer would determine whether the conversation would end here or not.

"Used to be our next-door neighbor, but she moved. I've asked Deb that same question and got told it was none of my business. That worries me, too. I suppose she's got someone else to agree to do it—and for free."

"You really gotta talk to a lawyer, Sid," Louie said firmly. "She's going to yank you around and yank you around about this money—that you don't even have—and she's going to use Colley to do it."

Sid turned again toward Jay. "So, you see, I got the divorce, nice and legal, paid for it, and now I'm being screwed. Maybe you ought to make up with your old lady."

Jay did not want the conversation to focus on his problems, but he wanted to try for one more piece of information. "My wife's seeing somebody, too. He works in the same place she does. I don't know if I could sue him or anything if we really do get a divorce."

"Wouldn't try that. You can't get very far with that 'alienation of affections' stuff anymore—courts don't allow it," Louie offered, finishing his second beer.

"Don't know where this guy works—if he works—that my ex-wife is seeing," Sid added. "Someone at work said he heard a rumor that the guy had served time once. Asked her and she got real mad. Probably doesn't matter, as long as he doesn't hurt her or Colley." Sid drained his glass.

Jay picked up his tab, slipped some bills onto the bar on top of it, and stood. "Thanks for letting me join you. And for the advice. Sure sorry about your not being able to see your son. You got any options other than spending money on the lawyers and going back to court?"

"I won't do that, yet," Sid answered, taking out his wallet to pay. "She'll probably come around, unless this money thing is a bigger deal with her than I'm figuring."

Jay stuck out his hand to Sid. "My last name's Berg. Jay Berg. Maybe I'll see you both in here again."

Louie was paying his tab. Sid took Jay's hand. "Mine's Hartman. Maybe we will. Good luck with your problem."

Jay left the bar ahead of them and got into the van. All evening, he was thinking of what he could do next about the house. When he got home, he opened a drawer in his tiny kitchen and found a pad of sticky notes. He put the pad in his lunch box, along with a marking pen. He set his alarm for 5 a.m. He wanted to be at work again early the next morning.

CHAPTER EIGHT

ON FRIDAY, JAY arrived at the job site early. He gambled he would be ahead of everybody else by at least fifteen minutes, and he was right. He drove down the road, past the field where the crew parked, and past the brick house. No one was in the driveway, and there were no signs of life there, as usual. After a quarter of a mile, he turned the van around and drove south again. Except this time, when he came to the driveway, he turned in and drove straight to the front door of the house.

After he parked, he opened his lunch box, took out the pen and pad, and wrote something on the backside of the first sticky note, just below the sticky part. He got out of the van, looking carefully around him. He saw a couple of cars driving north on the road but otherwise no one in sight. He walked over to the far window. It was about five feet off the ground — too high to see into but not too high to reach. With his right hand, he quickly lifted the small scrap of paper with the adhesive and stuck it in a corner at the bottom of the window. He had no idea how well the glue would hold against the glass, but he couldn't think of any other way to do this.

He looked around again and did not see anyone observing him, so he walked hurriedly back to the van, got in, and drove down the driveway. In two minutes, he was pulling into the field and saw Carlos driving in just behind him.

"Morning," Carlos called pleasantly when he saw Jay. Jay nodded to him and fell into step beside him as they moved toward the storage shed.

"How much longer are we gonna be working this stretch of road?" Jay asked.

"I think the trenching should be done by Monday night. If we lay pipe Tuesday and Wednesday, we might be able to move up a quarter of a mile or so on Thursday. Do you wish to get out of holding the sign next week?" Carlos turned to look at Jay, who realized the offer was a friendly one.

"Nah, I'm fine. Just asking. Hope the weather holds." He waited for Carlos to unlock the shed and took his sign. Counting today, he would have maybe three more workdays to be within sight of the house. Well, he had decided one thing. No matter what happened today, he would go to the sheriff's office on Saturday. With any luck, his brother-in-law, Vic, would be off duty and Sheriff Carlson would be on.

Since Becky's car wasn't in the field, Jay walked to his station and stowed his bag. At five minutes before start time, he saw the Elantra. But apparently Carlos was assigning Becky to the trenching detail because he saw her disappear toward the south end of the road and figured he wouldn't get to talk with her until their lunch break.

He was right. At 11:30, she came trotting up the road, and when she saw him, she had a grin on her face.

"Hi," she said, a little out of breath. "Sorry I didn't get here earlier, but I was running late this morning. Had to stay up to do a little research."

"And?" Jay asked, smiling back at her.

"Well, Carver Billingsley died two years ago. His estate is all tied up in the courts. It's not even clear who will end up owning the house, but it's in the estate right now. So, I don't know who would be selling it. This morning, I got a message from my friend Lillie. She was able to do a little checking on the phone number on that 'for sale' sign. She said the number hasn't been assigned for more than 12 months." Becky took a swallow of water from the runner's bottle she carried on her belt.

Jay turned to glance at the house and then turned back to Becky. "Thanks. I don't know where we go from here." He decided not to tell her about the sticky note—at least not yet.

"Are you going to tell the sheriff?"

"Maybe. I was just hoping to have some more information." Even to himself this sounded lame, so he added, "My brother-in-law is the deputy, and I don't have much confidence in him, plus he doesn't like me. But the real sheriff is a good guy." He paused. "How about I think about it until tomorrow and then I'll call you or text you and tell what I've done. Is it all right to call you?"

"Sure! But be careful with the law—they may not believe you if it sounds too crazy. Ben always says they hire the dumbest ones to be county cops. Anyway, I'm usually home all day, but I might be out in the morning doing errands. If there's anything you need me to do, I can probably do it. And maybe you'd like to share a pizza or something tomorrow night?"

Jay rapidly calculated what his Saturday would be like. He would spend the morning helping Alex in the orchard and then see if Emma needed any help. Tim's game was at three. He might get invited to a family dinner.

"I'm fine if we make it kind of late. My son has a ball game tomorrow. I'm not sure what's happening afterwards. How about I call you about eight and see where we go from there? If you're hungry before that, go ahead and eat." He knew this didn't sound very gracious, but it was the best he could think of at the moment.

"Fine with me. I'll wait to hear from you." She clipped the water bottle back on her belt and started off down the road. When she was about twenty feet away, she turned and gave him a little wave.

By three o'clock, cumulus clouds were forming in the west. By three-thirty, the first drops of rain started, and Carlos gave the signal to take the signs down. Jay hated to leave since nothing was happening at the house, and he felt sure his sticky note would get washed off the window by the rain. As he started down the road to return his sign, the first streak of lightning cracked close by. Jay stopped and looked back at the house. Just then a huge clap of thunder broke over the fields. Jay couldn't move. He was getting drenched, but he had the strongest premonition he had ever had in his life. He stared at the house.

He saw the wave. Just a little motion, right to left. And again, right to left. The hand at the window withdrew. Jay could no longer see if his sticky note was on the window, but he knew what he had written: "I'm here. Wave if you need help."

CHAPTER NINE

HE GOT INTO the van, where, of course, the seat was wet because he had left the windows open. He started it up and headed directly to the county sheriff's office. "If I have to deal with Vic, I'll do it," Jay told himself. Some child—or person—was in that house and in trouble. This was what he had to do.

He pulled into the parking lot outside the office twelve minutes later. Only one car was in the lot, and Jay couldn't tell if it was Sheriff Carlson's or one of the deputies. When he got inside, he saw that his luck had run out for the day—sitting at the desk, with his fingers poised over a computer keyboard, was Deputy Sheriff Vic Bartle, Emma's brother and Jay's brother-in-law.

"Someone pee on you?" Vic asked, looking up. Jay realized that rain was dripping from his hair, and he brushed a hand through it.

"Something like that," he answered in a level tone, debating now whether to tell Vic anything or just turn around and leave. He remained standing. "I've seen something at work. I need to report it."

"So? Where you working these days?" Vic straightened up in his swivel chair and pointed at a chair for Jay to sit in.

Jay looked at the chair and finally sat down. It looked to Jay like maybe Vic had lost a couple of pounds. His hair also looked shorter than Jay remembered. "I'm on a road crew, working on Route 23, Frog's Run road. We're laying sewer pipes. Ran into some trouble last week, so we've been in sort of the same spot for a couple of weeks. I'm mainly holding the sign."

"And you saw something over there? What is it—a wild boar?"

"No, but there's a vacant house on the road—with a 'for sale' sign in it. No one ever comes to look at it, at least that I can tell. It's got high windows on the front, several of them. Three times in the last week, I've seen something in one of the windows. It looks like a human hand, like someone putting his hand against the window. Kind of a small hand." He looked directly at Vic, who was looking back him with a look Jay took to be more puzzled than sarcastic. Vic pulled out a yellow pad and picked up a pen.

"Anybody else seen this hand?"

Jay thought about that. Had Becky been with him when he had seen it? No, he realized, she hadn't.

"No, and I haven't been drinking." He needed to say that to Vic at some point, knowing what Vic would probably suspect.

"Hmm," Vic mumbled absently, writing a note. He looked up. "Can you give me the exact dates and times you saw this, ah, hand at the window?"

Jay had expected the question and gave Vic the information. He did not mention his two nighttime stakeouts or the note he had written this morning and the waving hand later.

"And you say you haven't seen anyone come to the house?"

Jay hesitated. He could mention seeing the car that came both nights while he was watching the house from the woods. But then he would have to explain why he was spying on the house and did not come to the sheriff's office earlier. Plus, what could he say he saw? A dark-colored sedan with no license plates? That might make it sound as if he was making up the whole story, and Vic wouldn't believe him — if he did, in fact, believe him now. "No one while I've been working," Jay said carefully.

"You got the exact address?"

"There's no mailbox, but it's the only brick house in the last mile before you get to Route 7, and it's next to a farm with a white farmhouse that's number 178."

Vic was punching up something on his computer. "We've got no complaints about anything in that neighborhood — nothing going on there, at least recently." He looked up at Jay. "What, exactly, do you want me to do?"

Jay began to feel foolish. He wished that Becky at least had been with him once when he saw the hand. "I thought you and Sheriff Carlson should know. Could be some child in there. Maybe you could stake out the house?"

Vic looked at Jay for a minute, sighed, and stopped typing on his computer. He wrote something else on his yellow tablet and then looked up again. "Sheriff Carlson's up at the hospital for three days — annual checkup. So, we're short-handed until Monday. And it's probably a prank — or you're seeing things. But just in case, I'll set up surveillance on the house. If we see anything, we should be able to get a warrant to go in. You tell your road crew boss or buddies about this?"

Jay did not want to involve Becky, so he said, "No, I just came here to tell you."

"You call me if you see anything else. You don't work on Saturdays, do you?"

Jay shook his head. He got up to leave.

"How's Emma and the kids?" Vic asked, an edge of sarcasm creeping into his voice. He knew, of course, about the separation.

"They're fine. Emma got a raise at the factory. Tim's playing good ball this summer. He works on his conditioning—even runs every morning. I see all his games."

Vic grunted but did not comment. Given their past relationship, Jay found this almost friendly.

"And how's Louise?" Vic had been divorced for years, but Louise, a local potter, had been his on-again, off-again date for a long time.

"She keeps busy," Vic said, coming around the desk. He went to the door, opened it, and peered out. "Stopped raining," he informed Jay. Clearly, Jay was being dismissed. He took the hint.

"Thanks," he said and moved past Vic, making no attempt at a handshake or even eye contact. He pulled the door closed behind him. He felt deflated. Now the sheriff's office would take over, and he might never know what happened at the brick house. Well, that was what he had wanted, hadn't he? He wondered how soon they would send someone to watch. Would whoever was in the house be all right until then? Would a deputy see the hand and get a warrant or just get one anyway on the strength of Jay's report?

"This is really none of your business now," he reminded himself. He had a full weekend to look forward to, and there was still time this afternoon to drop by and see the children. Emma wouldn't be home from work yet, but Arlene, the daytime sitter in the summer, would be there.

Chapter Ten

WHEN HE GOT to his house, however, he saw no vehicles in the driveway. He got out of the van and went up to the front door, which was locked. He opened it with his key and called out for Tim, but there was no answer.

Jay guessed Arlene took them to Lake Bee. Both children liked the small lake and park fifteen minutes from their home. This summer, Lynn was taking swimming lessons; Tim was already a strong swimmer.

Jay felt let down. Finally, he decided to go to the Brick Bat and have an early supper and a beer. He could turn in early and get ready to help Alex first thing in the morning.

Friday night at the Brick Bat attracted more than the usual share of customers. Jay hated eating at the bar because it was the noisiest place. He found a small table for two, tucked back near the door to the kitchen. After the waitress took his order, he sat with his first cold Heineken and thought about the events of the past week. He wished now he had quizzed Vic about when they would have surveillance on the brick house and what they would do if they saw something going on. "Guess I'll find out eventually," he concluded. Just then Sid Hartman walked over to the table.

"Got room for one more?" Sid asked, smiling.

"Sure. Where's your buddy?"

"Louie's working swing shift. Thought I'd come in for an early supper. Looks like you might be doing the same?"

"Yeah. Gotta help a friend early in the morning, and then my boy has a baseball game in the afternoon." As soon as he said this, Jay was sorry since it would obviously remind Sid of his son, so he added, "You seen Colley since we were in here before?"

Sid shook his head. The waitress stopped by to take his order for a Bud. When she walked away, Sid said, "My ex is still holding out for more money. I'm going to follow Louie's advice and get a lawyer next week if I can't persuade her this weekend to let me see Colley." Sid pulled out his wallet. "Here's a picture of him. He's a cute kid, and smart, too."

The somewhat blurred snapshot showed a small boy with short, curly blond hair, holding on to the leash of a small dog and laughing up at the camera. "Took this the day before his last birthday." Sid paused and drank slowly. "I miss him."

"And you don't really have any idea where he is?"

"Well, I'm pretty sure she sent him to her mother—she lives in Florida. He likes it there."

The waitress came and took their orders—both for hamburgers.

"Did I hear you tell Louie you've never really seen your wife's new boyfriend?" Jay had drained his first beer and signaled for another.

"Just pulling up in his car one time. Colley calls him 'Uncle D'—whatever that means. I avoid the subject with Deb, except she keeps telling me what a 'great guy' he is—I know she's just trying to rub it in." Sid paused and looked down at his glass. "I guess money was always the bad thing between us. She likes nice things—wanted me to work two jobs or get a better one—wanted things we couldn't afford. It split us up—that and some other things. Anyway, we never knew exactly how much my dad had or if he was going to leave us anything. Turns out he never made a will, and I'm it as far as inheriting, but now they're probating the estate, so it will be awhile until I see any money. I think it'll be a nice amount, but probably nothing like Deb believes. And I know she thinks I'm holding out on her."

Their hamburgers arrived, along with two more beers. They ate for a while in silence. Finally, Sid said, "Think you said your wife's seeing somebody, too. You know him?"

"We worked at the same plant, but I didn't really know him. Can't tell how serious it is at this point, and my boy doesn't say much—and his little sister's too young to notice."

Sid took another sip of his beer. "Louie's been a good friend through all this. And it's funny, because his younger brother used to date Deb—that's how we met. I knew Louie and hung out with him. Eventually, I met his brother's girlfriend, and that was Deb. His brother, Mike, was pretty PO'd at me for a while, but he got over it." He paused. "We were married seven years. Guess I could have done some things different, but it's too late now."

Jay finished his burger first and pulled out his wallet. The waitress had left their checks on the table. He put down some cash. "Well, I'm going to go home and catch up on my sleep—get up early tomorrow. I really hope you work things out about Colley." He reached over the shake Sid's hand.

"Probably see you in here again?" Sid said, trying to smile but looking like he could have used Jay's company a little longer. Instead, he got up and started for the bar. "Think I'll watch the ball game for a little while. It was a good one last night."

Jay left and got into the van. It was only 7 o'clock. He decided to drop by the house and see the kids. He didn't want to admit it, but not having found them home earlier had worried him.

CHAPTER ELEVEN

H IS TRUCK—NOW EMMA'S—WAS in the driveway when he got there. He parked behind it and walked up to the porch, where all three of them were sitting, eating popcorn. "Dad!" Lynn yelled, running down the steps to meet him. Tim followed her, while Emma stood up but did not come down the steps.

Jay gave both children big hugs. "Hope I'm not interrupting anything! I came by earlier but you guys were out."

"We went to the park and the lake with Arlene and it rained, but we went swimming anyway, and then we had hot dogs, and we came home!" Lynn explained, out of breath. Jay gave her another hug.

"Hello, Emma," he said, sitting down in the porch swing. He remembered when they had bought it five years ago. Sometimes, after the children were in bed, they used to come out here and hold hands. He wondered if she remembered, too.

"Have you eaten?" she asked him, not smiling but not looking annoyed either.

"Yeah. And I'm going to turn in early tonight so I can help Alex early in the morning, but I just wanted to stop over for a few minutes."

"You're welcome to stay as long as you like," Emma replied, "but I may be going out. Arlene's coming back at eight."

Jay's good mood evaporated. "Well, I'll throw a few balls with Tim and then be on my way." Tim reappeared from inside the house with his mitt and ball. They went out to the back yard, and Lynn came to watch them.

After fifteen minutes, Jay said, "Your pitching's really improving, Timmy. I think you should have a shot at a pitcher's slot next year if you keep practicing." His son gave him a big smile. Lynn had already gone back to rejoin her mother.

Tim ran into the house to stow his glove and ball. Just as Jay walked through the living room to the front porch, he heard Emma's cell phone ring. He hesitated. Should he continue to the porch or give her some privacy? He decided to look at a magazine until she was finished, but the front door was open and he could hear clearly. After a few seconds, he heard her say, "You mean you can't come at all? Not tonight?" There was a silence, and then she said, "No, don't call me tomorrow. We're busy. I'll see you Monday."

Jay got up from the sofa and walked slowly out to the porch. "I'll be going pretty soon," he said, noticing that Emma was staring straight ahead with her lips pursed. *That always means trouble,* Jay thought. Lynn was in the front yard playing with her red wagon.

"You don't have to leave on my account. I'm not going out after all," Emma said in a low voice, not looking at him.

"All right." And then, because he could not resist, he asked, "Were you planning on seeing Patrick?"

Emma turned to him. Still keeping her voice low, she said, "Yes. On his schedule, of course. And now I'm not." Jay didn't say anything. He didn't want to show her that he felt like he just won something.

Emma looked down at her phone, which was lying on the little table next to the empty popcorn bowl. "He's done this a lot lately." Without another word, she picked up the bowl and walked inside.

Jay got up and followed her. When they got to the kitchen, he put a hand on her right arm, very lightly. "I'm sorry," he said.

She turned and gave him a bitter smile. "I'll bet you are!" But she sounded more sad than angry.

Just then, Tim bounded down the stairs. "Dad, can we go and get ice cream? I'm still hungry. We can bring some back for Lynn and Mom."

Jay glanced at Emma. "Go ahead, but you have to be home by nine o'clock—big game tomorrow," she reminded him.

"Thanks, Mom, I know!"

"Well, let's go then," Jay said, giving Tim a pat on the back. He turned to Emma. "It may be dark before we get back, but I won't keep him out too long."

CHAPTER TWELVE

J AY DID NOT want to admit it, but he had been thinking of driving by the brick house tonight to see if Vic's surveillance was in place. Now that he and Tim were going for ice cream, he could make a short detour.

"Tim, would you like to see where I work? There's lots of neat equipment there."

"Sure," Tim answered enthusiastically.

"We started trenching here," he pointed out to his son, as they turned on to Frog's Run Road.

"Do you run any of the big diggers?" Tim asked curiously.

"Not yet, but I will. And what I do is real important for safety—I handle the traffic flow. You know, stopping the cars when we have only one lane they can drive on, and then starting them up again." He hoped this sounded important enough to Tim.

When they got to where the diggers and the trenchers were parked, Jay pulled into the field, and they got out so Tim could look at the equipment. They spent ten minutes with Jay explaining what each machine did and describing how they all worked together. Finally, he said, "Look, it's almost dark, and I want to drive up to the end of the road. I'll show you where I sit when I eat my lunch. Then we'll get the ice cream and get you home."

In the half mile between the equipment depot and the curve in the road that would lead to the brick house, they encountered no traffic. The sun had set twenty minutes earlier, and the twilight was melding into dark. The moon was not yet visible. Jay took the curve slowly, glancing into the woods where he had been on stake out two nights. There was no sign of anyone there or on the road itself. He wondered if they would see a sheriff's car as they got to the house.

Tim suddenly sat up taller beside him. "Look, Dad! There are flames coming from that house!" Tim strained against his seat belt and pointed across his father's chest. Jay rammed on the brakes and stared at the brick house. He didn't see anything in the driveway—no car, no truck, but he clearly saw tongues of fire leaping up from the middle window. He shoved his foot onto the accelerator and took the turn into the driveway as fast as he could.

"Tim, you stay in the van. Do NOT come inside, you hear me?" he yelled at his son, who looked startled but only said, "Yes, Dad," as Jay hit the emergency brake, turned off the engine, and jumped out of the van. He ran for the front door. It was locked. The windows were too high to climb through even if he could break them. He ran frantically around to the back of the house. Near the back porch lay some two-by-four planks, and under the porch he saw the top of a ladder. It was small, wooden, old, and he did not know if the boards were rotten, but he had to try. He picked it up and ran back to the front yard.

Tim was out of the truck and dragging the old iron jack from the back of the van toward the middle window. "Here, Dad, you can break the window with this!" he shouted as his father came around the side of the house.

Jay didn't have time to worry about Tim's being out of the van. He put the ladder in place and grabbed the jack from his son's hands. He climbed up two steps on the ladder. "Stand back," he said to Tim, who moved but not far. Jay heaved the jack at the window, and it broke. The heat poured out, and he knew he could not get in safely. "Tim, look for a hose!" he said, and he saw Tim run to the side of the house.

Jay grabbed the ladder and moved it to the window where he had seen the hand. Again he climbed, and again he heaved the heavy jack against the window. This time, the glass fractured in two places but did not break. *What if someone is in there, right under this window, and the glass cuts him?* Jay thought, but he had no other choice. He reached back with the jack and threw it with all his weight against the window. Out of the corner of his eye, he saw Tim running back with the nozzle of a hose in his hand. Water was streaming from the nozzle. "Aim for the flames," he shouted at his son, who was already positioning himself under the middle window and aiming the hose up.

The window in front of Jay shattered completely on Jay's second try. He dropped the jack. He knew he couldn't climb through the broken glass safely. He tore off his shirt and placed it over the bottom of the window frame where, fortunately, most of the glass had fallen away. He did not know how far the drop was to the floor below, but he had to risk it. He took a deep breath and dropped down.

There was no light in the room. It took Jay a few seconds to see anything. When he could see, he made out a cot in the far end, what looked like a small table next to some other box-like structure, and—in the corner, a small figure cowering against the wall.

Jay ran to the child—or whatever it was. The figure was curled up with its head down on one hand, which was hugging its knees. The other hand seemed to be behind its back. Its feet were bare. Then Jay realized some kind of tether bound the left hand in back and was hooked to a metal bar high up on the wall. Jay touched the small head with the short, black hair. "It's all right. I'm the one who wrote you the note. The house is on fire. You gotta come with me now!"

The head came up, and Jay could see it was a child—a little boy, he assumed. Slowly, as if in a trance, the child held out his free arm to Jay. "I knew you would come," the tiny voice said, and his eyes closed.

Jay grabbed his penknife from his pocket and hacked away at the tether, which seemed to be made of leather. After what seemed like minutes, it broke. Picking the child up, Jay debated whether to try to get out the front door. Then he realized the flames could be spreading in that direction. The better way out seemed to through the window and down the ladder—if he could manage it.

"I have a ladder outside your window," he said in a firm voice. "I'm going to let you down to the ladder, and you have to climb down. It's only five steps, and my son is going to be waiting for you down below. He will help you." Jay fervently hoped that Tim was still fighting the flames and watching for him. He felt the child's head nod against his chest.

Jay lifted the child up over the shirt covering the windowsill and onto the first rung of the ladder. He couldn't see after that and hoped the child was hanging on and starting down. Jay turned back into the room. He needed something to stand on to get himself out. He grabbed the little table. It was just the right height. He got himself up on the sill and looked down. The child was on the last step before the ground, and Tim was holding out his arms to him. "It's okay, I'm here!" he heard Tim say. Jay knew that even if he lived to see Tim pitch a no-hitter in the World Series he would never be as proud of Tim then as he was of him right now. Jay climbed down the ladder.

"Get in the van!" Jay yelled at Tim, taking the little boy from him. They both ran. The hose lay on the ground, still spouting water, but the flames in the middle window were out. Jay opened the back door on the driver's side and placed the child in the seat, rapidly fastening the seat belt. "Tim, get in the other side and sit next to him," Jay commanded, and Tim got in.

For once, the van started up immediately, and without even turning on his headlights, Jay sped down the driveway. They were just a few yards from the road when Jay saw a dark sedan approaching from the south.

He remembered his headlights and turned them on. The sedan had no lights. Jay thought he could see just one person—the driver—but he could not be sure. He didn't know if it was the car he had seen at the house before, but he thought it was. He had only a couple of seconds to decide whether to turn toward the oncoming car or away from it. If he turned right at the road, at least the other driver could not immediately follow him. If he turned left, he could easily be followed. Jay turned right.

The sedan was slowly approaching the driveway and now suddenly swerved slightly left on the narrow road. Jay gripped his steering wheel and made for the ditch, which he knew from hours of standing in that very spot was not deep. But the ground was soft from the rain, and the van started to slide. Jay wrenched the wheel to the left to stay on the road, and at that moment, he saw the large dump truck coming straight at him. The last thing he remembered was yelling at Tim to get his head down. Then there was a sharp pain, and then—nothing.

CHAPTER THIRTEEN

HE'S COMING OUT of it." Jay heard a voice and opened his eyes. The light in the room almost blinded him, and he put up a hand to shield his eyes. He felt bandages on his head and on his hand. He looked around.

A man in a white coat was leaning over him, and behind him stood a woman in a pink uniform. "How are you feeling?" the man asked.

"Where am I?" Jay asked, relieved that he could talk. And then, with a hazy memory coming back, "Where is my son?"

"You're in Western General Hospital. You were in a crash with a truck. You've got some injuries, but you're going to be fine. We've contacted your wife and she's on her way here. I'm Doctor Gilbert, and this is Ann Levy, our head nurse on this floor."

Jay tried to sit up and felt a sharp pain in his back. "My son—my son was with me—and another child, in the back seat. Are they all right?"

Dr. Gilbert and Ann Levy exchanged glances. "Mr. Berg, when the rescue squad found you, you were alone in your van. No one else was with you. The driver of the truck was also hurt—he's got some cuts and bruises, but he's going to be all right, too. You say your son and another child were in your van? Are you sure?"

Jay moaned. He could remember everything now, right up to the moment of trying to get the van back onto the road. He didn't remember the van being hit, but he knew the boys had been in the back seat.

"Yes, yes—they were there. There was a fire at a house nearby. My son, Tim—he's ten—he helped me rescue this little boy. I don't know his name. Please tell them to go and look for the boys—maybe they were hurt and wandered off into the woods. I work around there. There are woods." Jay lay back, exhausted emotionally and physically.

"I'm going to contact the police," Dr. Gilbert said reassuringly and left the room. Ann handed Jay a plastic glass with cold water and a straw in it. "Drink some water—you'll feel better. I'm sure they'll find your son. The police may already have found him."

Jay looked up at her. "How bad off am I?"

"You have a concussion, cuts on your face and on both arms and hands—especially the right one—and you may have hurt your back, but your airbag deployed, and there aren't any broken bones. We'll probably keep you here a couple of days, though. We've notified your wife—we found your name on your driver's license. Is there anybody else you want us to call?"

Jay thought about Alex and Carlos and decided he could have someone get in touch with them later. He started to say "not now" when Emma burst into his room. Her face was white, and she was fighting back tears.

"Jay, where is our son? Where's Timmy?" She came right up to his bed but did not touch him. He could see the fear in her eyes.

"Emma, I don't know. I don't know. The police are going back to where we had the accident. He must have wandered off into the woods. There was another little boy with us. We rescued him from a burning house. They were in the back seat. They had their seatbelts on. I don't know what happened. A car swerved at me. I swerved, too, and next thing I knew a big truck was in front of us. Emma, I'm so sorry—I'm so sorry."

He reached for her hand with his bandaged one, and she finally took it, tears now streaming down her face.

"Mr. Berg, I'm going to leave you and Mrs. Berg alone now, but you push this button right here if you need anything. As soon as we hear anything about your son and the other child, we will let you know. I'll call the highway patrol and the sheriff's office myself if we haven't heard anything in an hour or so." Ann Levy paused and then left the room.

"Emma, there's things I haven't been telling you," Jay said when the door closed behind Ann. "I'd like to now." Emma pulled up a chair and sat down close to the head of his bed. There were two glasses on his tray, and she helped herself to a glass of water. "Who's staying with Lynn?" Jay asked, feeling the pain in his back again.

"I took her next door. She'll be all right tonight. I told her it was a special sleepover." Emma closed her eyes and tried to hold back the tears. "Tell me the things you haven't been telling me."

Jay started at the beginning, when he had first seen the hand. The only parts he left out were his conversations with Becky and the fact that she went on the stake out the second night. He didn't have anything to be ashamed of about Becky, he thought, but he didn't see how it would do any good to tell Emma. He did tell her that he had reported the whole thing to Vic that afternoon.

Emma listened closely to everything he told her. Then she was silent for a few minutes. Finally, she said, "If you think that car you saw was the same one you saw before, do you think whoever was driving it had something to do with the boys' disappearing?"

Jay decided to be honest. "Yes. I think it's possible. Emma, I think he may have taken both boys, but I don't know why. I don't even know if it was the same car I've been seeing at that house. I don't know why that little kid was in there or what is happening. But, yes, I think he might have the boys."

Emma closed her eyes. "I'm going to call Vic."

"I'm sure the sheriff's office knows all about it by now, but maybe Vic can give us some information we can't get otherwise."

Emma pulled her cell phone out of her purse. "I'll try his cell and then his house. It's late." She looked at her watch. "Almost midnight." She dialed the first number. After four rings, she got voice mail. She tried Vic's house. Same result. At both numbers she left the same message. "Vic, it's me. Jay's been in a car crash. He's at Western General. He had Timmy with him, and Timmy's missing. We need help. Please call me."

Jay took her hand again and she did not pull back. "We may have to wait for some information," he said, and she nodded. They stayed like that for a while, waiting for someone to come and tell them the nightmare was over, that it was all a misunderstanding, but no one did.

CHAPTER FOURTEEN

HE NEVER INTENDED for anything like this to happen. Hiding one boy had proved difficult and dangerous. Hiding two might just be more than he could handle. He'd made a phone call for some help and gotten some advice. Now, he'd given both boys pills, and they were sleeping. Fortunately, he knew the people who owned this house where he was now, and they would not be back for at least a month. Their basement had only two small windows that you couldn't really see into for the dirt. That's where he had the boys now. He'd had this place ready, just in case, but he had hoped he wouldn't have to use it. Tomorrow, he would get more supplies—water, peanut butter crackers, and some rope. The chemical toilet was already there. He needed to figure out a way to tie the older one up—or at least make sure the door was secure. It had a lock, but the older one might be able to figure a way out. He needed to think about that.

What if I'd gotten to the house too late? he wondered for about the twentieth time. He could see from the road that something was wrong—a broken window and maybe damage to the roof. And he smelled smoke. If there was a fire, he knew it was probably his fault—he was sometimes careless about putting out his cigarettes, and maybe one of them was left smoldering in the trash. He had been planning to take out the trash that evening.

He'd recognized the van when it pulled out of the driveway—the same van he'd seen nosing around before. And he saw the crash with the dump truck. Before anybody else could get there, he'd gone up to the van, meaning only to find out who was in it—and he'd found the driver slumped over, bleeding, and both boys in the back, scared but all right.

He was wearing his disguise, like he always did, but he had to think fast. If the older boy saw him take the younger boy out of the van, the older boy would tell—and he might be able to describe in some detail what he saw. This was not a time to take a chance, so he hit the older boy over the head with the gun and grabbed the younger one. He couldn't carry them both, so he loaded the younger one into his car, tied him up, and then came back for the older boy. He tied him up, too. The older boy came to on the way to the "safe" house, and he started yelling. But the windows of the car were up, and the house was isolated, so when they got to it, there was no one around to hear.

He reminded himself that it was all about the money—that was what he should concentrate on. Maybe he could even get more money, maybe a ransom for the older boy, but that meant more planning than he could do by himself right at the moment. "Bastard shouldn't have interfered!" he said aloud, thinking of the van driver as he climbed the steps out of the basement. He had to get back and cover his tracks, be sure his alibi worked. He thought about going back to the brick house to clean it up, but he knew there might be law enforcement people there now, investigating the crash scene. He reminded himself that he was very careful not to leave fingerprints anywhere. But it was better to wait until very late tonight—or very early in the morning to go over there, and even then he'd have to watch his step. If there had been a fire, maybe it would take care of any stray evidence anyway.

Another thing he was certainly going to do early in the morning was contact her and tell her to push the issue of the money. If it came through, then he would return the little boy. That left only the other one to consider. He didn't know if he could get a ransom for him, and it might be too dangerous to try. *May just have to get rid of him,* he thought, as he drove slowly away from the "safe" house and back to the highway. He'd think about that more tomorrow.

CHAPTER FIFTEEN

FTER ANOTHER THIRTY minutes, during which Jay intermittently dozed, Ann Levy came back into the room. She carried a pitcher of fresh cold water. "How are you feeling?" she asked Jay?

"About the same, except my head hurts more now," he answered.

"I'll bring you some pills for your head. I've talked with an officer at the Highway Patrol office. They say they have people on the scene of your crash, along with a sheriff's deputy, and so far they have not found your boys. They know to call the desk here on the floor if they find out anything." She moved closer to the bed. "I need to take your temperature now," and she slid a thermometer under Jay's tongue. After a few seconds she looked at it. "Just a couple of degrees above normal—that's good."

Just as Ann was pouring Jay a fresh glass of water, Emma's cell phone beeped. "It's a text from Vic—he's on his way here."

Ann looked at Emma inquiringly.

"Vic's my brother. He's the deputy sheriff in this county."

"Vic Bartle? Is he the one who broke the drug ring several years ago?" Ann Levy sounded surprised.

"Yes," Emma replied. "He's very good."

"Then I'm sure he will be a big help to you," Ann said with a smile. "I'll bring the pills for your headache and then be back again in about half an hour to check on you."

Vic came through the door ten minutes later. He hugged Emma and squeezed Jay on his undamaged arm. "Louise and I were out to dinner, and we went back to her place. I turned off my phone for a little while or I would have gotten your call. I'm so sorry about this. I have Armillio Sanchez back at the crash scene, and there are Highway Patrol people there, too. They have orders to report anything to me as soon as they find something. Jay, can you tell me exactly what happened?"

Jay had taken the pills Ann brought, but his head still throbbed. He went through all the details of how he and Tim visited the brick house and what happened. Vic listened carefully and took notes. A couple of times he sighed, as if to say, "you stupid SOB," but he didn't make any comments until Jay was finished.

"We're short-handed," he said then, turning to Emma. "I had Armillio scheduled for surveillance at the house, only he had to answer a call on a domestic dispute. Then he was supposed to be at the house by ten. It's my fault that we didn't have someone there sooner. But I want you both to know I will do everything possible to help you find Timmy—and this other child that you say was there."

Jay winced. *That you say was there*. What did that mean? That Vic didn't believe him? That Vic thought Jay had been drinking or was deliberately lying? Jay's feeling of some relief that Vic would help began to vanish. Should he tell Vic about Sid Hartman and his missing son? No, that was a private matter between Sid and his wife and none of Vic's business, unless, of course, Sid declared his son a missing person. But in the picture of Colley that Sid had shown Jay, Colley clearly had blond, curly hair. And the picture was recent. The child Jay found had short black hair. So who was the child in the brick house?

Jay saw Vic glance at his watch. "I need to check in with Armillio and then get the duty schedule for tomorrow revised," Vic said, rising from his chair. "Emma, I'll call you as soon as we know something. Did you drive here? Can I take you home? I hate to have you be alone tonight."

Emma looked down at the floor. "I drove, and I'm all right. Lynn's at the neighbors. On my way here, I had a call from Patrick. He heard about the crash on the scanner he keeps in his car. He told me he'd meet me at the house when I got home from the hospital. He was worried about me." She said this last bit in a defiant tone, as if to forestall anything Jay might say.

But Jay simply let his head fall back onto the pillows and closed his eyes. He couldn't deal with thoughts of Patrick McNaughton tonight. And, in a way, he was glad someone would be there for Emma.

"You can both go. I'm feeling better. I think these pills are working. But, please, call the nurses' station as soon as they find Timmy!"

Emma bent down and gave him a very light kiss on the cheek. "They'll find our son, Emma," Jay said, but his voice was weak. Vic gave him another squeeze on the arm. "Of course we will—and soon, too."

As they were leaving, the night nurse, a petite, dark-skinned woman with a name badge identifying her as Paula Arapahoe, came in with a basin of water and towels. "Time for a bed bath for you!" she said cheerfully. "I guess they didn't want to do anything but bandage you when you first came in, but I'll take good care of you now." She reached over and gently pulled down Jay's hospital gown. "You were in a car crash, right?"

Jay groaned slightly as she touched his left arm. "Yeah."

"Sorry—I didn't mean to hurt you." She worked with a damp wash-cloth for a few minutes on his face and neck, and her touch felt gentle to Jay. When she came to his left shoulder, she rubbed more vigorously and then frowned. "You've got a black smudge on your shoulder and I can't get it off—at least not with this soap. Do you remember if oil or something spilled on you?"

Jay tried hard to remember anything after the crash but he couldn't. "I took my shirt off to cover some glass on the bottom of a window I had to break. There was a fire and smoke, but I don't know where the black stuff would have come from." He tried to think—had he touched anything in that room before lifting the child out? Not anything that would have touched his shoulder. The only thing that touched his shoulder was the little boy—his head, anyway. And realizing this, Jay struggled to sit up straighter in bed and to concentrate. "Can you tell if it's some kind of dye?" he asked, trying to look down at his own shoulder, but his neck hurt when he did this.

"Could be. I'll get a little rubbing alcohol. Back in a minute."

The nurse returned with two small bottles. "One of these should work."

"If it's hair dye, would you know that?" Jay asked. The nurse looked at him, puzzled.

"Well, not necessarily, but I use rubbing alcohol myself when I'm coloring my hair to get off any tell-tales—you know, color spots that I don't want." She moistened a piece of cotton and rubbed. She lifted the cotton to show him—it was covered in gray-black. "That did the trick!" she reported and resumed giving him the rest of his bath.

Jay felt more relaxed now, but his mind was racing. *If that little boy had his hair dyed, maybe it was blond before*? It was a long shot, but maybe if that was true it was Colley, Sid's son. Tomorrow, Jay knew he would have to make a decision. He would have to find Sid and tell him about the little boy in the house—the little kidnapped boy who might be Colley.

Chapter Sixteen

LOUIE GOERTZ LEFT the factory after midnight on Saturday with his pay in an envelope and plenty to worry about. The shift had gone well, but his wife was home with the flu, and he hoped that's all it was. Then, he had tried three times during his breaks to call Mike, and each time he got voice mail. "He's up to something," Louie concluded, although knowing his younger brother, it was probably just a hot date. Mike was a bachelor, and Louie didn't think he lacked for company.

The last time he saw Mike, Louie noticed Mike was wearing very fancy boots that he surely could not afford on a Quik Mart clerk's salary. Louie sighed and gunned the car up to seventy. No cops were on the road this time of night. Louie also hadn't spoken to Sid since Thursday, and he knew Sid was really feeling terrible about not seeing Colley. Louie had asked around the factory if anybody knew a good lawyer who might be able to help Sid, and he'd gotten a couple of names. He'd call Sid on Sunday.

The drive home took half an hour, so he turned on an all-night music and news station. A few minutes into the trip he heard the news roundup. He didn't pay much attention until the announcer mentioned a crash in the next county and something about missing children who had been in the vehicle. Then Louie heard the name of the driver: Jay Berg. "That's the guy who moved in on us at the bar!" he realized, with some surprise. "I'll have to tell Sid about that. Seemed like a nice enough guy, although maybe a little nosey. Hope he gets those kids back." That made two people he knew who had missing children. Louie shook his head. "Not a good world for some people."

In spite of getting home late, Louie got up early to make breakfast for his wife, who was feeling better. After breakfast, he called Sid.

"Hey! Glad you called," Sid said. "I'm going over to see Deborah this morning, and if she won't tell me where Colley is, I'm going to tell her I'm getting a lawyer first thing Monday morning."

"I got a couple names of good ones for you," Louie reported. He read off two names. "Couple guys at the factory recommended them both. Got something else to tell you, too." He repeated the newscast he had heard coming home.

"I just ran into Jay at the Brick Bat last night and had a hamburger with him!" Sid said in amazement. "He was going to go home early and get up to work in some friend's orchard. I can't believe this. Did they say where he is now?"

"Western General, I think."

"Maybe I'll go over there after I see Deborah. Poor guy. Now we've both got sons missing."

"Give me a ring later," Louie said, reaching for his coffee cup. "Gonna do some yard work, and maybe we can catch a beer. Let me know."

§ § §

It was midmorning. Sid sat in his kitchen for a few minutes, trying to make a decision. He picked up the phone and called his ex-wife. No answer. "I'm coming over between 11 and noon. We need to talk," he said after the beep. He grabbed a couple of "Field and Stream" magazines that he thought Jay might like and took them out to his car.

When Sid got to Western General Hospital, he found Jay sitting up in bed, watching television. He was in a double room, but the other bed was unoccupied. "Hey, I didn't expect to see you again so soon!" Sid said, trying to sound cheerful as he entered the room. He held out the magazines. "Thought you might like something to pass the time." He stood awkwardly at the foot of Jay's bed while Jay stared at him with a peculiar expression that Sid couldn't read. Maybe he shouldn't have come?

"Sid," Jay finally said, still staring at him. "Pull up a chair. I'm *very* glad to see you."

This puzzled Sid even more, but he moved a chair near the head of the bed. "I hope you're not in too much pain. Louie called me this morning because he heard on the radio late last night that you'd been in a wreck. And that you had kids in the car. Was it your boy and someone else? I'm really sorry."

"Sid, I need to tell you about something." Jay unfolded all the events that led up to his accident. He made the whole story as short as he could, finishing with the stain that Nurse Paula had found on his shoulder.

"And you think that boy could be my Colley?" Sid asked incredulously when Jay had finished.

"I don't know."

Sid stood up and started pacing the room. "I'm going over to see Deb

60

right now. I'm going to force it out of her where Colley is. I thought she had maybe sent him to his grandmother in Florida. He likes it there. But maybe she doesn't even *know* where he is!" He turned back to Jay, fear and anger alternating in his eyes.

"Look, Sid," Jay said, hoisting himself as high in the bed as he could. "Maybe you ought to see a lawyer first—like Louie wants you to. If Deb is dealing with some low life, maybe you want to know what your rights are before you talk with her."

"Colley *is* my right. He's my son! She has to tell me where he is. If she thinks he's in trouble, she'll come around. I know her. She's not really bad—just greedy sometimes. And she loves him as much as I do." Sid's voice broke on these last few words, and Jay looked away.

"Well, call me when you've talked with her. And I'll call you if they find my son and the other child. It may not be Colley, but at least when they find the boys, we'll know."

Sid nodded and walked back to the bed. He put a hand on Jay's shoulder. "I'm gonna call you or come back here as soon as I know something. If you get out today, is there somewhere I can find you?"

Jay reached for the pad of paper near the bed and wrote down his cell phone number and Alex Rosen's address. "I'll probably be here tonight. They might let me go home tomorrow." He wanted to say something comforting for both of them, but he didn't know what it could be, so all he said was, "Thanks for the magazines."

Sid nodded and got up to leave. He glanced at Jay as he got to the door. Jay's eyes were closed. "Maybe he's thinking about his son—just like I'm thinking about Colley," Sid thought to himself. He winced. Two of them with missing sons didn't make things better.

CHAPTER SEVENTEEN

TIM KNEW FROM watching television shows that someone gave him drugs. His tongue felt dry and his head ached. One of his arms was raised above his head, and his wrist was tied with what looked like a long leather bracelet to a metal bracket in the wall. His arm ached, too. When he stood up, that relieved the pressure on his arm, but he couldn't quite reach the bracket with his other hand. As his eyes became accustomed to the dim light in the room, he saw there was a box with crackers on top of it and a water jug. He could reach the jug, so he took a long drink. Then he saw the little sleeping bag near the box and realized he was not alone. It took a few minutes for him to remember what had happened after his dad had loaded him into the back of the van, but then it all came back to him.

He watched the child on the sleeping bag for what seemed like a long time until the child finally made a noise and turned over. His eyes opened. Tim moved as close to the child as he could. "Hi. I'm Tim. What's your name?"

The child cringed and looked around, but he did not cry. Tim decided to keep trying. "Someone brought us here. We got you out of a burning house, and then my dad crashed his van. He'll be here to get us, though, real soon." Tim wanted to believe this, but he wasn't as sure as he tried to make his voice sound. Still the child said nothing. Tim realized that the little boy was not tied up. *I wonder if he can get me undone?* Tim thought.

"We've got crackers here. I'll toss you one," Tim said, reaching for the food on the box and throwing a peanut butter cracker in the general vicinity of the sleeping bag.

The child reached for the cracker and gobbled it, looking around him. Then he looked directly at Tim. "It's that man!" he said in a louder voice than Tim would have expected.

"What do you mean?" Tim asked, puzzled, wondering if the little boy was referring to Jay.

"It's that man who took me to that house, Uncle D," the child said as if explaining something easy to someone very simple. "He's mean. He left me in the dark." The child looked around, perhaps seeing his new surroundings for the first time. "It's dark here, too."

"Did he *kidnap* you?" Tim asked, realizing that he still hadn't gotten an answer to his first question.

"I don't know. I live with my mom, and he took me away from there because he told me we were going to see my dad and we were playing a game. My mom said it was okay. I don't know where she is now." For the first time, Tim sensed that the child was going to cry.

"Well, we'll get out of here. My dad will come for us. And you didn't tell me your name."

The child stood up and walked toward the food and water. "I'm Colley."

"I'm Tim."

The little boy regarded him soberly. "You helped me get out of that house. Was that your dad with you?"

"Yes, it was. He's very brave, and that's why I know he is looking for us and will come and get us." Tim suddenly realized that his father might have been seriously hurt when the van crashed. Now he needed to fight back bad thoughts. "Look, I think there is something we can do before that man gets back. I'm tied up and you aren't. If we take the food off that box, you could stand on it and maybe untie me. Do you want to try?"

Colley nodded, and with surprising speed, moved the food and water to the floor, dragged the box over to Tim, and with a helping hand from Tim, climbed on top of it. He could easily reach the thong and the bracket, but however it was attached, he could not get it loose. "I can't do it!" he said, whimpering.

"Let's try to find something we can use to cut that with," Tim replied, thinking that there would not likely be anything in this basement. He looked around in the dim light. One of the small windows near the ceiling had a crack in it. "Colley, I want you to move the box over to that window. Then, I'm going to take one of my shoes off and give you my sock. I want you to put it over your right hand. Then, I want you to take my shoe and climb on the box. You're going to punch out that window that has the crack in it with my shoe. Do you see it?" Tim pointed.

Colley nodded, and again without saying anything, he moved swiftly to do exactly as Tim instructed. He climbed up on the box, and with Tim's sock on his right hand, he used Tim's shoe to hit the window as hard as he could. A small pane of glass fell to the floor.

"You did great! Now, climb down and pick up that little bit of glass with your sock hand and bring it here to me."

Colley held out the piece of glass carefully in front of him as he crossed the room. Tim pulled the sock off of Colley's hand and with Colley's help maneuvered it onto his own left hand. Then he grasped the piece of glass awkwardly and began sawing at the leather thong just above his wrist. At first, Tim didn't see that he was making any progress, but after ten minutes he saw that the glass had penetrated the leather. In another ten minutes, the cut was deep enough that Tim yanked back on it with all his force and the strap broke. Tim fell backwards, and his back hit the concrete floor hard, but it was the best pain that he had ever felt. "I'm free!" he said excitedly to Colley, who just looked at him with widened eyes. Then Colley threw his arms around Tim's waist and hugged him hard.

Tim had no idea what time it was, but he knew the man would be back. They needed to escape if they could. Now that he was free, he walked around the room. There were the two small windows—probably too small to push Colley out of, although that was a possibility. There was a door that was not only locked but would not budge when Tim leaned hard against it and pushed. There was the box, the toilet, Colley's sleeping bag, an old blanket off in a corner, and nothing else that Tim could find. He had carefully placed the shard of glass on top of the box.

Tim looked down at Colley, who was standing very close to him. "Do you think you could crawl out that window if we got all the glass out? Then you could run for help."

The little boy stared at the window for a few seconds. "I think so. Can you get me up there?"

He's brave, Tim realized but wondered if this was really going to be the best solution. Realizing that their kidnapper would probably notice the already broken glass anyway, Tim decided that pushing Colley through the window was worth a try. "Get me that blanket," he said, pointing to the corner.

Colley ran back, dragging the blanket. Tim climbed onto the box and took the blanket. He covered his body and hands with the blanket as best he could and began banging at the cracked window with his shoe. The glass was old and brittle; it shattered easily. Soon, a few shards of glass lay on the floor around the boys. Tim knocked out as much of the glass around the rim as he could. Then he placed the blanket at the bottom of the window. He got down off the box and faced Colley.

"Listen. Here's what we're going to do. I'll lift you up. You see if you can climb through. If you get out, run as fast as you can to the nearest house and find somebody and tell them we've been kidnapped. If you see the man coming, hide in the bushes or something. I'll be right here, and I'll try to hit him over the head."

"What if I can't get out?"

"I'll just push until you do!"

He climbed back up on the box and reached down for Colley, who felt heavy in his arms. Tim boosted him as high as he could and felt some of the weight go off his arms as Colley squirmed onto the window ledge. He held his arms stiffly at his sides and poked his head through the opening. Tim strained to reach as high as he could, grabbed Colley's legs, and pushed. Colley didn't budge. "I'm stuck!" he yelled, and Tim prayed that the man was not within hearing distance.

"No, you're not—try to get an arm through and grab something."

Colley wriggled until his right shoulder and right arm disappeared outside the opening. Tim grabbed Colley's ankles and gave a huge shove. Nothing. He tried again and suddenly Colley was through, his feet not quite outside kicking in the air. "Run!" Tim said but not too loud. He could see Colley's legs going upright and his feet almost flying along the ground.

For the first time, Tim realized that it must be morning because light was streaming in. He pulled the blanket away from the window and got down from the box. Now that he was alone, he felt relieved that Colley was out, but he had no real idea what to do next. If the man came back now, he would probably be very angry. Tim needed to make a plan.

§ § §

Colley ran away from the house as fast as he could. For a few minutes all he could see were the overgrown weeds and scraggly trees he was stumbling through. Tim told him to find a house. Finally, he saw some kind of building off in the distance to his right. As he got closer, it looked like a house with a couple of little buildings near it. There had to be people there. They would help. He got closer. He could see a road, too, so maybe someone in a car would help him. He started to run toward the road, and then he saw the car. He couldn't be sure it was the bad one, but he thought so. He ran back into the bushes and started to creep toward the house.

The car sped off down the road. He waited under a pine tree for what seemed like an hour and was about to run toward the house again when he heard barking. A dog—a big one. Colley was frightened of dogs, even though his dad told him over and over again that he shouldn't be. He missed his dad. Tim had a dad who would come for him. Colley couldn't remember how long it had been since he had seen his own dad. *Why doesn't he come for me?* he wondered, but he knew that right now he was on his own.

The barking got closer, and then he saw what looked like a giant black and tan animal. Colley looked around frantically. The nearest place he could see was one of the small buildings off to the side of the house and much closer to where he was hiding. The dog was running toward him. He ran faster than he ever had in his life and reached the shed just as the dog got within a couple of yards. Colley tried the lift-up latch on the door and it opened. He flung himself inside and pushed the door shut just as he heard the dog's claws scrabbling on the wood. He was safe. It was dark, except for one small window, and it smelled like dirt and other things he could not identify. He sat down and drew his knees up to his chin. He could see garden tools now and some brown flowerpots and some gunnysacks. It was stuffy in the shed, and suddenly he felt awfully tired. He moved over to the gunnysacks and lay down. The dog was still barking. *Tim's dad will come and get me—or maybe my dad.* This was his last thought before he fell asleep.

CHAPTER EIGHTEEN

J ust tell me where he is—that he's safe!" Sid was raising his voice now to his ex-wife. Deb backed away from him but stayed standing in the living room.

"I *told* you—I'm not going to tell you where he is until you promise me my share of the money." She grabbed a thick strand of her blond hair and pushed it back from her face.

Sid knew that Deb did not react well to threats or to his anger. "Sit down," he said, trying to think of a new strategy. They had been at it for ten minutes, and he was no nearer finding out about what she had done with his son than he had been when he got to the house. He decided to try reasoning with her.

"Deb, I've told you—I don't know how much Dad left, and it won't be mine for maybe a year—it's in what they call probate. Can't you understand that?"

She turned away even though her chair was facing him. "I don't believe you. I have a friend, and he said you'd probably get a bundle. You can promise me half now and I'll let you see Colley."

"I can't promise you half of what I don't have, but I will promise to be fair with you and Colley when the courts let me know how much it is. But you don't have any right to keep Colley away from me! At least tell me where he is. Is he with your mother?"

Deb refused to look at him, but she shook her head "no." Sid felt defeated, angry, and scared at the same time. What if the little boy who disappeared with Tim was really Colley? He had to play his last card.

"If you won't tell me, I'll hire a lawyer and have you hauled into court. You're in violation of my visitation rights. So, you tell me *right now* where he is and let me see him, or I'm walking through that door and making a phone call."

"You're just threatening me. It's the weekend. Who you gonna call on the weekend?" Now she looked at him defiantly and tossed her stray strands of hair back over her shoulder.

"I'm leaving," Sid said in a low voice and started toward the front door. "If I don't hear from you exactly where Colley is in an hour, the next call you get is from my lawyer."

Sid did not have the courage to go back and face Jay, only to tell him that Deb wouldn't tell him anything, so he used his cell phone to call Jay's hospital room. After he delivered his message, he felt completely defeated. Jay had said he would be too weak to leave the hospital today to help in the search, although he told Sid he would check himself out in the morning. Sid wondered if there was anything he could do in the meantime. He decided to go to the house where his son had apparently been held. Jay had told him how to find it. But when he got there, a police car was parked in the driveway and there was yellow tape blocking the doors and windows. Sid turned around and drove home. He had to find Colley, but how was he going to do that? Maybe he and Jay could do something together, but Jay wasn't in very good shape right now. Sid sat at his own kitchen table and tried to think.

§ § §

Tim was trying to figure out what to do ever since he pushed Colley out the window. No one came, and now he worried that maybe the kidnapper found Colley and was going to bring him back to the basement.

He looked at the blanket, lying rumpled on the floor. Could he stuff it under the door enough to make it hard for the man to push the door open? Even if he could, so what? He could delay somebody's getting in the room by blocking the door, but then how was he going to get out? He was simply too big to crawl out the little window Colley had used. His dad had once shown him how to take a door off its hinges when they were going to paint it. The door to the basement room opened in, which meant the hinges—two of them—were on the inside. Tim thought they looked rusty, and he knew it was hard to work with rusty metal. He didn't have anything to use to pry up the hinge pins anyway. So he couldn't get out that way.

Maybe he could pretend to be hurt—or asleep—when the man came back and then somehow hit him over the head. But with what? He could, maybe, use one of the pieces of broken glass to cut the man, but wouldn't that only make him mad? Tim knew that time was running out. Either his dad or the police would find him, and he would be safe, or the kidnapper would come back and Tim would be on his own. He tried to think what his dad would do.

And then he remembered a time when he came home with a bloody nose because he got in a fight at school. "Why did you fight?" Jay asked him.

"Because the guy tried to take my lunch!"

"Well, maybe it would have been better to give it to him. Always think about what it is somebody really wants. If he's bigger than you or can hurt you, sometimes it's just better to let him have it to protect yourself."

Now, Tim asked himself what the kidnapper might want and the answer was easy: money. But how could Tim help get the money? Well, if he told the right kind of story, maybe he could. At least it might get him out of this basement. He pulled up the blanket, folded it, and sat down to think up what he could say when the kidnapper came back.

CHAPTER NINETEEN

H E REPLAYED THE voice mail message from Deb, and it did nothing to ease his mind. Her voice sounded frightened and angry. "Sid's been here, threatening me, so you better tell me what we're gonna do next. And I want to see Colley today." He had reassured her before he took Colley that he was taking the boy to be with some older people out of the county. The people were friends who had grandchildren and would take good care of Colley. He would have a good time with them.

He checked the text message that came through a few minutes ago from a different source. "Let the older boy go." That's what the text message said. *If I let him go, he'll talk, and, anyway, I'll bet I can get more money for him,* the kidnapper thought to himself and sent back a question but got no answer.

Now it was early afternoon as he drew up to the house where he had left the boys. He pulled up behind the garage and waited ten minutes. Nobody came, and the house could not be seen from the road. He got out of the car, but instead of going in the back door and directly down to the basement, he decided to walk around the house once — just to see if anything looked different. Within his first ten steps, he saw it: the broken window at the top of the basement wall. Several pieces of glass, both large and small, were lying on the ground, meaning the window had probably been broken from inside.

So it wasn't somebody kicking it in, he thought. "The little bastards must have tried to get out!" He turned and ran toward the back door, unlocked it, and vaulted down the stairs. He half expected the basement door not to open when he unlocked it, but he pushed it open on the first try.

The older boy was sitting on the box where the food had been. The man looked around frantically. "Where is he?" he yelled and then realized he should keep his voice down in case anybody was outside. He reached Tim in two steps and shook him violently by the shoulders. "You tell me where he is or I swear I'll kill you — and him, too."

Tim was shaking and looked frightened, but he looked up at the man, who had on tinted glasses.

"I broke the window and he climbed out. He was scared. I told him to run. But you have me. My dad has money, lots of it. He'll pay you to get me back."

"Oh, yeah, smart guy? And what does he *do*, this rich father of yours?"

"He has some money that my grandpa gave him, and he works extra jobs sometimes. He keeps it in a safe in our garage that my mom doesn't know about—only me. He said he'd keep it for me and give it to me some day." The man stood close to Tim, looking down at him. Tim tried to keep eye contact, but after a few seconds he hung his head.

"How much does he have in that safe?"

"It's more than twenty thousand dollars."

"He's got a cell phone, doesn't he?"

Tim nodded, looking up again. "You want the number?"

"Oh, yeah, smart guy, I want the number, and I'm gonna text him. Then I'm going to tie you up again so you can't give me any more trouble."

Tim recited the number of his dad's phone. The man booted up his phone and programmed the number in. Tim had looked at the screen to be sure the man got the number right.

Tim's voice sounded less frightened now. "But if you leave me here, won't somebody notice the broken window? Maybe they'll call the sheriff or try to break down the door."

The man hadn't thought of that, or the fact that Tim could probably yell loudly, and he really didn't want to have to gag him since he had once heard from an ex-con friend about a gagged prisoner choking to death. *This little bastard is smart,* he admitted to himself. *It shouldn't be so damn hard just to get some money for these stupid kids.*

"I'm gonna board up the window you knocked out, and you'll be tied up so good you won't be able to knock out the other one. You can yell all you want, but there's nobody around." With that, he grabbed Tim by the arm and dragged him back to the spot where he had been tied up before. The piece of leather was shorter now, so the man took off his own belt and rigged it up so it fit tightly around one of Tim's wrists, with the belt buckle securely fastened to the hook on the ceiling.

"You don't get food until I get back, and I better get the money or I won't come back at all!"

§ § §

Tim watched as the man grabbed the door and swung it shut after him. He heard the sound of a padlock being clicked into place. Only now did Tim allow the tears that had been stinging in his eyes to overflow. But his scheme worked. The man believed the story about the money and the safe. Once, Tim heard his parents discussing how much a good used truck would cost—twenty thousand dollars. That was how he picked the number. Of course, there was no safe—and no money.

He sat still for a few minutes. His right arm already hurt from being held above his head. Then, slowly, he reached into his pocket with his left hand and felt the small piece of jagged glass he had kept there for the last hour. He knew he would have to wait until he saw the man boarding up the window and heard the car leave. Then he could start cutting the leather belt.

CHAPTER TWENTY

WHEN THE KIDNAPPER got outside, he quickly took some small boards he had in the trunk of his car and placed them over the broken window. He didn't have any nails, but he pushed the boards in tightly as best he could. At least no one could see in, and the other window was so dirty you couldn't see much through it, either.

As soon as he got back in the car, he turned on his phone again. He wasn't ready to send a text to the kid's father yet, but sure enough, he had another voice mail from Deb. This one arrived about five minutes ago, and she sounded more frantic. "D, you gotta call me now. I want to know where Colley is. And Sid's getting a lawyer. We *gotta* talk." He turned off the phone—he knew that when it was on it could be traced, meaning people could find him. He had bought two pre-paid phones to use now, just in case, but he knew he would have to keep checking messages on his regular phone.

He gunned the engine and drove down the driveway. He wanted to get away from the house and think about how he was going to find Colley. He certainly did not want to admit to Deb that he didn't have him now.

Where would a little kid run to from here? he asked himself as he reached the main road. There weren't many other houses around. Would he have gotten out to the road and hitched a ride? He might have been too scared for that, so where would he have gone?

He could see the outlines of some buildings down the road to the left and back into the woods. It was the only place he could see, and maybe that's what Colley had seen, too. He'd try there first. If people were home, he would make up some story about watching the boy for his mother and the youngster running away. If nothing came of that, he'd drive around and look for any other houses close by. He'd do this for at least a couple of hours before calling Deb—or anybody else. He'd work out a ransom demand for the older boy—maybe—after he got Colley back.

§ § §

The dog was still outside the storage shed. When Colley woke up, he could hear the dog panting. It was getting very stuffy inside the shed, and Colley wanted to get out. Somebody must be up at the house by now, somebody who could help him. He stood up and walked toward the big door; maybe he could open it just enough to see out. He reached up and lifted the latch, pushing on the door very slowly.

The big dog was lying in front of the door. When he heard it open, he turned his head toward Colley, and to Colley's amazement, gave a small whine and began wagging his tail. Colley was still afraid, but he opened the door another couple of inches. He could see the house quite clearly. Could he run up there without the big dog hurting him? He did not know, but just as he was trying to think this through, he saw a car pull up to the house. It was too far to see who was in it, but if these were the people who lived in the house, surely they would help him. Colley pushed the door all the way open. "Nice dog," he said in a small, uncertain voice and began to run.

The black and tan dog stood up, stretched, and began to lope after him. In a couple of bounds, he was running ahead of Colley. And then, suddenly, the dog stiffened, stopped, and started to bark. Colley stopped, too. A man was getting out of the car. The man had a gun, and he was pointing it at the dog. Colley knew who the man was. He began to cry.

"Now, you come here, Colley," the kidnapper said. "You come here nice and slow and I won't have to shoot the dog or you." The man started to crouch down and hold out his left hand—the one without the gun—to Colley.

As soon as he saw the left arm being extended, the dog leaped. He covered the few feet between himself and the man in two seconds, not enough time for the man to realize what was happening and get a shot off. The dog hit the man's chest and sank his teeth into the man's neck. Then, he bit the man's right arm until, with a yell, the man dropped the gun. The dog was now on top of the man on the ground. Colley, who felt he couldn't move his feet five seconds ago, took one final look, turned, and ran into the woods.

CHAPTER TWENTY-ONE

S ID'S CELL PHONE rang just as he was about to make a call to the first lawyer whose name Louie gave him. Even if it was a Saturday afternoon, he could leave a message. He half expected the caller now to be Deb, but then he heard Jay's voice.

"Sid, he's definitely got my son, and he's asking for a ransom. I think Tim must have told him I have money. But I don't. I need to get out of here. My van's smashed so I don't have wheels. Can you come and get me?"

"What happened? How do you know he's got your boy?"

"He sent me a text on my cell, saying he had Tim, and then he called me. Just a few minutes ago. He told me how Tim was dressed so I'd know it was for real. Sid, I can't just lie here knowing he's probably got both boys. He said if I called the law, I'd never see Tim again. We gotta do something!"

"Did he say anything about Colley?"

"No."

"Did you tell him you'd meet him or leave the ransom somewhere or what?"

"I told him I was in the hospital and people were in the room. He said he'd call back with instructions in an hour and then hung up. I tried calling back the number he called on but it just rang."

Sid slumped in his chair. He could pick up Jay, but what good was that going to do? Still, he knew they could work better together than alone.

"I'll be there in half an hour. I gotta make one phone call first, but I'll come for you. Wait in your room."

Sid rubbed his eyes. Then he dialed the number of his former home. Deb answered on the second ring, like maybe she'd been waiting for a call.

"Deb, it's me. I didn't mean to threaten you today. I'm sorry. But Colley may be in danger. Deb, you gotta tell me who you've been dating, where he lives, how to get a hold of him. He may have done something with our son—and maybe with another boy, too."

Sid heard a little cry at the other end of the line. "What do you mean 'done something'? What are you saying?"

Sid gritted his teeth and lowered his voice. "I mean he may have kidnapped two children, and Colley is one of them. There was an incident. I can't tell you all about it now, but the police are involved. And I need to know about your boyfriend. If he's not involved, he won't get in trouble. If he has our son and has done anything to him, he'll be in plenty of trouble. If you want, I can bring the sheriff over and you can tell him everything. Or you can tell me. Now."

There was a long silence on the other end of the line. Then her voice came through, very faintly. "It's Mike."

"Mike *who*?"

"You know—Mike Goertz. We've been dating for a while now."

"And you're telling me *Mike Goertz* has kidnapped my son?" Sid was raising his voice.

"No! He didn't kidnap him. He said he'd keep him safe while you came through with the money—that you were such a bastard you wouldn't do it if we didn't hide Colley. I told Colley it was all right to go with Mike, that it was a game." Her voice choked, but she was beginning to sound angry, now, too.

Sid gripped his phone so hard his knuckles hurt. "Deb, I need his phone number right now. His address, too. I'm going to call the sheriff, and then I'm going to find Mike—and our son. If he calls you or sends you any messages, you call me before you tell him anything—do you understand?"

Silence again for a few seconds. Then: "I'll call you first. But he wouldn't do anything to Colley! He loves him and me, too!" Now she sounded defiant, and Sid did not know if he could trust her. He played his last card.

"The police could put you and Mike away for life if anything's happened to Colley. Just remember that. Do what I told you. Give me his number and his address now."

When he got to the hospital, Sid found Jay dressed and sitting on his bed with a sack of his personal things next to him. He looked pale but somewhat relieved to see Sid. "Did you find out anything?"

Sid closed the door to the room. "I found out who took Colley, and he's probably the one who's got both boys. Name's Mike Goertz, actually Michael Devlin Goertz—sometimes goes by 'D.' He's Louie's younger brother—used to date Deb, like I told you the other night. He's been in trouble before, but I never thought he'd be dumb enough and mean enough to try a stunt like this. I made her give me his cell phone number, and I've called it in to the sheriff's office. Had to leave a voice mail message. Maybe you can call your brother-in-law. I tried Mike's phone, too, but no answer. I didn't leave a message. Maybe he's ditched his phone and switched to another one. Are you ready to get out of here?"

Jay got up slowly, and they walked to the elevator, then out to Sid's car. As soon as they were in the car, Jay said, "I'm gonna call Vic. I know that bastard said not to call the law, but Vic will help." He got through to Vic's personal phone on the third ring.

"Vic, it's me, Jay. The kidnapper called me—he wants a ransom for Tim. I think I know who he is. Sid—that's Colley's father—talked to his ex-wife, and it looks like her boyfriend, Mike Goertz, may be the one who was hiding Colley, so he may be the one who has Tim, too."

"Did the man who called you give you a name or any type of identification?" Vic was all business now.

"No, and could be it's not this Mike, but I have the number on my cell phone that he used when he called me, and Sid's got a number for him, too." Jay read off both numbers slowly.

"I'm going to follow this up immediately. You and Sid go to his place or yours and let me know where you are. If the kidnapper calls you back, stall for time and get as much information as you can. We'll be tracking the cell numbers. I'll call you as soon as I find out anything. And I'll call Emma, too."

When Jay repeated Vic's instructions to Sid, they talked about what they should do. Neither of them wanted to go to an apartment and just sit, waiting.

"Maybe we could drive around and see if you could spot that car you think he's been driving?" Sid asked, knowing this was probably futile.

"Sure. Maybe he has the boys somewhere not too far from the house where I found Colley."

Sid knew that if they found Mike before Vic or the law did, the two of them would have to do something. Sid didn't say anything for a few minutes. Then he made their part in the plan clearer. "I've got a revolver in the glove box. I'll use it, if we have to." Jay nodded.

Chapter Twenty-Two

COLLEY RAN SO fast his lungs ached, but he was in the woods now, away from the house, the dog, and the bad man. He could see a clearing up ahead and he ran for it. When he got there, he saw the road and a field on the other side. At the end of the field he saw a big brick house. It looked like a nice house, and he started out for it.

The car picked up speed as it rounded the corner of the road. Colley ran almost directly in front of the car. The driver barely had time to swerve and hit the brakes. The car missed the child by inches. The child froze in the middle of the highway. The driver got out.

"Hi. Are you okay?"

Colley couldn't find his voice, but he nodded. He had never seen this person before, or this car.

"Let's get off the road." The driver reached out a hand and Colley took it. He walked with the driver to the car, which was off on the shoulder.

"Are you lost? Can you tell me your name?"

"I'm Colley Hartman. I'm trying to find my dad. I want to go home!" And with this, Colley felt a few tears roll down his cheeks.

"Well, we'll get you there. Can you tell me where you live?"

Colley recited his address.

"Good. I know where that is. Let's get in the car, and I'll take you right home. It isn't very far."

They drove in silence for a mile, and then the driver asked in a friendly voice, "How come you are out running around all alone? Won't your mother be missing you?"

Colley felt confused. Should he tell this stranger that he had been kidnapped? Was he being kidnapped again? Finally, he said in a small voice, "Somebody bad tried to hide me, but I escaped."

The driver's eyebrows went up. "Well, that must have been scary. We're almost at your place now."

Colley recognized his neighborhood two blocks from his house. He got up on his knees to look out the window. Now they were just a few houses away.

"Tell you what. Your mom might be worried if she sees a stranger dropping you off, so I'll just let you out here and you can run the rest of the way."

Colley didn't even answer. As soon as the car stopped and he heard the door unlock, Colley scooted as fast as he could and ran all the way up to his porch. He pounded on the door, and two seconds later when his mother opened it, he fell into her arms, yelling, "Mom, Mom!" Deb Hartman staggered back against the half-open door and then grabbed Colley. Now both of them were crying.

"Colley, Colley—how did you get here?"

Colley turned to see if the mysterious car was still out there, but when he turned around to look, he saw no one.

Chapter Twenty-Three

AFTER MIKE HAD fought the dog off and gotten back to his car, he was bleeding slightly from the bites on his neck and his arm. *Damn animal*, he said to himself. *Animal like that should be shot — maybe I'll come back later and do it.* He found some paper towels in his glove compartment and mopped up the blood with water from an old bottle on the floor in the back. The bites worried him less than the fact that he had lost Colley. How was he going to explain this? Maybe he could find him if he drove around in the area, but then that meant he couldn't get back to see about Tim and work the ransom problem.

It was time to send a text to Jay Berg and then call him. *Guy didn't say much*, Mike reflected, thinking about his contact with Berg, as he started down another unfamiliar road. Right now, he had to plan the details of the ransom. For a few minutes he debated with himself: was all this worth it for just twenty thousand dollars? But he was supposed to get a lot more — if he had kept Colley. Anger began to build in his mind. *I deserve something for all this work! So what if it's only twenty thousand — at least I can get that. I deserve that!*

He decided to spend a little more time looking for Colley. Driving slowly on the back road, he didn't spot anyone. A couple of trucks passed him, but he didn't see any children in them. After fifteen minutes, he gave up. He tried to convince himself that if Colley got away someone would find him, and no one could tie the boy to him. Deb had sounded pretty mad in that last phone call, and she might just tell someone he had taken Colley against her wishes initially. Of course that wasn't true — she had been quite willing. "But if she lies, I could say I was taking care of him and he got away from me."

Half an hour had gone by since he had called Jay Berg. "Time to give him a few instructions," Mike thought. He had finally worked out the details in his head, and he didn't need advice from anyone.

First, he was going to go back to the "safe" house, give Tim a sedative, and get him out to the car. Next, he was going to call Berg and tell him to bring twenty thousand dollars in unmarked bills by 7:15 p.m. to the old pumping station at Lake Charles, twenty miles away. He would tell Berg to leave the money in a gunnysack that would be outside the door of the station. Berg would then have to get back in his car, drive at least five miles away, and wait for another call that would tell him where Tim was. Mike planned to wait in the woods where he could see the road and the pumping station. Assuming no police showed up and the money was in the sack, he would call Berg back and tell him Tim was in a boat tied up at a dock half a mile from the pumping station. If anything went wrong, Mike planned to circle around, pick Tim up, and get out of there. Then, he'd try another tactic, although he hadn't yet thought through what that would be.

When he got to the vacant house, he parked behind it, unlocked the back door, and started down toward the basement. Right before unlocking the basement door, he stopped to listen. No sounds. Maybe the kid was sleeping or passed out. He seemed like a feisty kid, but he would be no match for Mike. He unlocked the door.

Because of the boarded-up windows, little light entered the room. Mike squinted at the place where he left Tim tied up and saw his belt strap dangling there. Something shiny lay on the floor. He bent down to pick it up, realizing it was his belt buckle. Then, just as he started to straighten up, he felt a crushing weight land on his back.

Tim got his hands in Mike's hair and pulled hard. He didn't make a sound, but Mike yelled and flailed around to try and get Tim off his back. Tim held on hard, but after a minute he started to fall. The next thing he felt was a sharp punch in the jaw.

"Bastard!" Mike yelled, picking Tim up around the waist. "I oughta kill you." Instead, he slammed the boy onto the concrete floor where Tim's head made a sickening thud. For a few seconds, Mike thought he *had* killed him, but he felt for a pulse and found it.

Damn, now I probably can't get any pills into him, he thought with disgust, but he realized that having the boy out cold would probably work just as well as a sedative. Without even bothering to tie him up, Mike lugged Tim's limp body up the basement stairs and loaded him into the back seat of the car. Before he shut the door, he took some of the rope pieces he had brought and tied Tim's hands and feet. He still did not want to use a gag and risk choking him.

Now he had to make the phone call to Jay Berg, and it was possible Tim might be able to hear. Mike got out of the car. He dialed Jay's cell phone number.

86

"You know who this is," he began, and without waiting for an answer, gave Jay the instructions. Then he said, "You got that?"

"I don't have the money! I need more time!" Jay's voice sounded faint and worried.

"Your little boy says you got plenty in that secret safe, so you go and get it. If that money in the sack isn't at the pumping station by 7:15, or if you bring any lawmen with you, you can kiss your boy goodbye." Mike rang off. So far so good. When Tim woke up, he would have to sedate him, but that shouldn't be too hard. He checked on the boy one last time—no movement—and started off toward Lake Charles.

CHAPTER TWENTY-FOUR

SID STOPPED THE car when Jay's phone rang. Now, they sat on the side of the road. Jay looked pale and was shaking.

"What'd he say to do?" Sid asked.

"Tim must have told him I have money somewhere—he talked about a safe. He wants twenty thousand in cash. By 7:15 tonight." Jay closed his eyes and lay back in the seat. "I need to call Vic."

But before Jay could punch in Vic's number, Sid's phone rang. First Sid just listened, and then his face started to flush. He half turned toward Jay, while he was saying, "I'm coming—I'll be there as soon as I can. Call the sheriff and tell him." He put the phone down and grabbed Jay's left hand, squeezing it hard. "Colley's home—he came home to Deb! Someone found him and brought him home. He's all right. He's safe."

"That's great, Sid. I'm gonna call Vic now, and I'll tell him. Can you take me home first? I may need transportation, and Emma can drive me."

Sid heard the pleading note in Jay's voice and realized that his friend still had *his* crisis going on. "We'll go to your place right now. You call Vic. I'm sure you'll get Tim tonight."

While Sid drove—a few miles over the speed limit—Jay called Vic.

"Vic, he called me back. The kidnapper. He wants money—twenty thousand dollars—I don't know where he came up with that number—out at the pumping station at Lake Charles by seven fifteen tonight. But Vic, I'm in Sid's car and he just got a call from his wife that his boy, Colley, is home. Some stranger found him and brought him home. What do you want me to do?"

Sid could hear Vic's end of the conversation clearly.

"You go home. I'll handle this. You don't have any money, do you?"

"No, I don't, and he said I wouldn't see Tim again if I didn't bring the money or if there were cops."

"I'll take care of it. I need to get two of my deputies lined up. I'll call you again in thirty minutes."

Both men looked at their watches. It was 5:15 p.m. They were half a mile from Jay's house. But when they got there, his truck was not in the driveway. Sid volunteered to go to the front door, where he rang the bell and knocked, but no one came.

Sid tried the door, too, and it was evidently locked. Sid ran back to his car. When he got in, he said, "No one home. Where to now?"

"My apartment. I have a friend I can call, or my landlord will help. One of them can drive me."

Sid nodded and sped off. He felt badly that he could not stay with Jay and help him, but his own son was home — at least with his ex-wife — and safe, and Sid wanted to see him more than he had ever wanted anything in his life. He was even ready to forgive Deb for ever agreeing to the stupid, dangerous scheme. Just so Colley was all right.

When they got to Jay's apartment, Sid helped him up the steps. "Sure you're gonna be all right here? You need me to come back"?

"I'll make it. You need to see Colley. I'll call you later and tell you what's happening. If you find out anything more about this Mike from your wife, let me know."

Sid grasped Jay's hand. "Thanks for rescuing Colley. He wouldn't be back without you. I can drive you later if you need me." Without waiting for any more conversation, Sid rushed back out to his car and drove away.

§ § §

Jay turned on one overhead light and sat down on the small sofa. He felt faint. He struggled to his feet, went to the refrigerator, and got a bottle of water. He knew he should call Emma, but he was afraid that she would panic about the ransom. What he really wanted to do was not call her until it was all over — and he hoped that would be soon. But he did want to call Becky. Suddenly, he wanted very much to hear her voice, to ask her to help, to rely on her. He dialed her cell phone number.

"Hello?"

"Becky, it's me, Jay," he began, knowing his voice was trembling. He told her as quickly as possible what had happened since late Friday night. Then, "I'm at my apartment. Can you come over? Pick me up? I don't have wheels, and I'm not sure I can drive, but I need to get out of here."

She did not question him but simply said, "I'll be right over." He felt relieved and a little better. He drained the water bottle. He knew he couldn't come up with twenty thousand dollars, but Vic would have an idea of what they could do. He waited for Vic to call and for Becky to come and get him.

CHAPTER TWENTY-FIVE

ECKY KNOCKED ON Jay's door ten minutes after he called. She gave him a quick hug. "Can you get the money?"

"No way that I know of, but I'm waiting for Vic to call back. He should any minute now. The sheriff's office probably has some way of getting cash temporarily."

"I could go to the bank—I have a little cash I could get out at the ATM. Would that help?"

Jay felt a lump in his throat. He took her hand and held it for a moment. "Thanks for thinking of that, but I'll have to let Vic decide what to do."

His phone chirped. "Hello?" A few seconds of silence, and then Becky heard him say, "But what if he's expecting to see *me*?" More silence and Jay frowning. Finally, "All right. Just call me when you know something, and I'll call you if he calls me." Jay leaned back and closed his eyes briefly.

"That was Vic. He doesn't want me to go to the pumping station or anywhere near Lake Charles. He's sending someone to check out this Mike Goertz's place. He says he'll also have two of his men in the woods, watching. He'll have one of them who is about my height and wearing a jacket, dark glasses, and a hat put a fistful of bills in the gunnysack in front of the door of the pumping station and then drive away. It's going to be real money. He thinks the kidnapper will fall for it when he opens the sack and sees money. They'll arrest him when he takes the sack and opens it. Then they'll force him to tell them where Tim is."

Jay paused. "I don't like it. What if this Mike knows it's not me putting the money into the sack? What if he does something to Tim before they arrest him? What if he won't say where Tim is—or maybe just kills him before he picks up the sack?"

Jay's voice was rising, and he felt ready to cry. He looked at his watch. It was almost six o'clock. It would take about twenty-five minutes to drive to the Lake Charles pumping station.

Becky faced Jay. "Have you tried calling him back on your cell phone at the number he called you from? You could say you need to have more time and some proof Tim is all right."

91

"Guess I could try that, but I don't think Vic wants me to do anything now but sit tight." Suddenly Jay stood up. "It's a good idea. He might give up some information about where Tim is now—or even let me talk to him."

However, when Jay tried to find the "incoming" call number on his phone and hit the "call" button, he saw a screen that said, "This number blocked." He hurled his own phone down on the rug in anger.

"To hell with it! Let's go to Lake Charles. We can park your car in the woods and find somewhere to hide so we can see the pumping station. If Vic screws up, maybe the guy will still call me—as long as he believes I've still got the money."

Becky pulled the keys to the Elantra from her purse. "I'll drive. We'll make this work. I just need to send a quick text. Ben was expecting me to call him about now—then we'll go find your son."

Jay headed for his fridge to get them both bottles of water. He saw Becky tapping out her message as he did so. Maybe Ben really was the jealous type. He felt a moment of guilt about not trying to reach Emma, but he thought it would be better to wait until he and Vic would have Tim, and the kidnapper would be in custody or maybe even dead.

He and Becky headed out the door into the warm evening. Jay carried the two bottles of water. He wished he were carrying a gun.

CHAPTER TWENTY-SIX

MIKE LOADED TIM—WITH hands and feet bound—into a small fishing boat that was tied up at an old wooden dock. Tim was conscious but groggy from the pills he was forced to take. He didn't have a gag in his mouth, but the kidnapper had tied some kind of bandana across his face so tightly that he could barely breathe. He didn't know exactly where he was. He felt scared. He was also worried about saying his dad had money, but maybe that worked because now the kidnapper was getting back into his car and driving away. *If he's going to go collect the ransom, maybe that means Dad found some money and he'll rescue me!*

Tim tried moving his hands. They were tied behind his back, and he couldn't seem to loosen the rope. He could wriggle a little in the boat, and he could move his legs and feet up and down. He tried kicking the floor of the boat to make noise. That worked, but he decided to wait for a while before trying anything else—maybe he wouldn't have to wait long.

§ § §

Mike looked at his watch. It was time to hide and see whether Jay Berg would deliver the ransom. An old, abandoned shed came into view—the one he checked out earlier. He parked the car under the crumbling roof and moved through the bushes to a spot where he could see the main entrance of the pumping station. Lying flat on his stomach on the ground, he raised a small pair of binoculars. He could see the empty gunnysack he had dropped in front of the door when he was on his way to put Tim in the boat. He waited ten minutes without seeing or hearing anything. Only one road led into the station, and he felt confident that no one was hiding anywhere else in the woods watching *him*.

Five minutes later, he heard what sounded like a car or truck coming down the road. He thought he heard a faint noise somewhere in the woods, too. He lay very still. He could not see much of the road because it turned sharply just before entering the small parking lot in front of the station. He heard the motor stop. The other noise he thought he had heard stopped, too.

A few minutes later, a man wearing a loose-fitting dark jacket, baseball cap, dark glasses, and jeans emerged on the far side of the pumping station. He was slightly bent over and occasionally looked around, as if checking for someone. He was carrying what looked like two packages, wrapped in brown paper. When he got to the door of the pumping station, he bent down to retrieve the gunnysack. He quickly stuffed his packages into it, turned around, and headed back in the direction he had come.

Within two minutes, a car engine started up, and Mike could hear it retreating down the road. He waited until things were quiet for ten minutes. He saw no movement anywhere in the part of the woods that he could see. Crouching slightly and continuing to look around, he moved toward the front door of the station. Then he paused. What if there were cops after all? He could take the sack and run to the car. Once there, he could open the door without anyone seeing him.

When he got to the gunnysack, he grabbed it, turned, and ran back fast toward his hidden car. Once inside the car, he opened the gunnysack and tore open the paper of the first package. Several one hundred dollar bills fell out. He rifled through the package—full of hundreds, and they all looked real. He tore open the second package—same thing. There wasn't time to count everything. He put the key in the ignition to start up. He began backing out of the shed, but the car barely moved and something felt funny. Without shutting down the engine, he leaped out. He couldn't see anything wrong on his side of the car, so he ran to the other side. Two flat tires. "Goddamn, goddamn!" he yelled, not thinking about whether anybody could hear him or not.

No time to fix the tires—and he didn't have two spares anyway. He grabbed his cell phone from the front seat, made sure his gun was secure in his right pants pocket, and closed the drawstring on the gunnysack. His plan, hastily conceived, was to run into the woods, in the opposite direction from the pumping station. He could come back for the car later. He had to call Berg and tell him where Tim was. And if there were cops around—although everything was going all right so far, except for the flat tires—he had to get away.

The voice somewhere behind him boomed out, "Stop!" He pivoted, reaching for his gun. He aimed it in the direction of the voice. A rustling sound moved toward him. He fired once and then twice in the direction of the voice and the footsteps. Then he started to run just as the next two shots rang out.

Chapter Twenty-Seven

Jay and Becky, crouching far back on the road where they could just see the pumping station, both jumped, startled, when the shooting started. The first thing that went through Jay's mind was what if the kidnapper had been shot and couldn't tell them where Tim was.

"Come on!" He grabbed Becky's hand and pulled her in the direction of the shots.

In less than a minute they saw Vic. He was kneeling over the body of a man near a black Chevy that Jay recognized as the one he saw going to and from the vacant house where Colley had been locked up. Vic turned when he heard them; he was holstering his pistol. Incongruously, Jay noticed that a button on Vic's uniform was missing.

"I thought I told you to stay home!" he boomed at Jay, struggling to his feet, but then his face relaxed a little. "I think we got him," he said, pointing to the motionless figure on the ground.

Becky stopped, but Jay moved closer and peered at the man. Blood was showing through his shirt, and Jay couldn't tell if he was breathing. "Is he dead?"

"He's got a pulse. I was gonna fire a warning shot when he grabbed the sack, but my gun jammed. Then he shot at me, so I had to use my gun. He missed. I didn't."

"Can he talk? He was supposed to call me and tell me where to find Tim!" Jay thrust his face inches from Vic's. "How are we going to find my boy now?"

"I have my deputies out looking. One of them planted the ransom so we could catch him red-handed. Then I sent them to scour the area. The boy can't be far. This asshole is too dumb to have done anything clever with him." Some of Vic's usual swagger was returning. "I've got to radio in for an ambulance." He made the call and then turned to Jay and Becky. "This guy is carrying ID sayin' he's Mike Goertz—that was the name you gave me earlier, so based on what we know, he's probably the kidnapper of both boys."

Jay stood motionless, looking at the body on the ground. He had a sickening feeling that Goertz wouldn't talk and Tim would never be found. "I've got to look for him — for Tim," he said, almost to himself. Out of the corner of his eye, he saw Becky had moved away toward the kidnapper's car. She was crouching down. Jay was pretty sure she was being sick.

Vic put a hand on Jay's shoulder. "If you want to ride with me, we can all look, or you can go home and I'll call you as soon as we know something," Vic assured him. "My deputies are good — they'll find Tim. And I've got a man searching Goertz's house and talking to his neighbors right now. I think I can get a helicopter from the next county sheriff's office to do aerial surveillance. Did he say anything to you when he called that might help us find Tim?"

Jay thought hard. No, there had been no mention of a location — or how far away Tim was. "If he hadn't found the money when he showed up, wouldn't he have had to get Tim again right away and take him some-place else?" Jay stopped, swallowed, and chocked out, "or killed him? So maybe he hid him someplace we wouldn't think about."

Vic looked at Jay curiously. He nodded. "Good thinking. Do you want to come with me or not?" So far, he hadn't acknowledged Becky directly. She had walked back shakily and was standing beside Jay. Vic addressed the question to both of them.

Becky looked at Jay. "Why don't you go with Sheriff Bartle? I can drive around wherever you both think I should go. Maybe we can cover more ground that way. With you, me, and the sheriff's men, we can maybe find him quickly." She tried to make her voice reassuring.

"We'll drive between here and Goertz's house — that's northwest," Vic announced. "Any vacant buildings or any spots that look like hiding places, we'll investigate. And my men will be in touch." Turning to Becky, he said, "you can drive in the opposite direction — there's plenty of barns and abandoned buildings around here, around the lake. I have my men covering the road east of here."

Jay listened to both of them. "I'll go with Becky, Vic. If you find Tim, he knows you, and he'll go with you. If he sees a stranger — even Becky — he might be afraid. I'll ride with her."

"Suit yourself. You got your phone with you?" Vic sounded annoyed. "Yes."

"Good. Get going. As soon as the ambulance comes, I'll start back toward his house. Call me if you see anything suspicious. He might have had an accomplice."

They all heard the approaching sound of a siren. Jay turned toward Vic. "Can you try to see again if he'll talk?"

Vic bent down toward Mike's head. "If you can hear me, raise you right hand," he said loudly. Nothing happened.

Jay stepped forward and stood right over Mike's body. "You got your money — now where is my son?" He didn't realize it, but he was yelling. There was still no response.

The ambulance was only a few yards away now. "Come on." Jay said, taking Becky's hand. "Call me!" he said to Vic. "Call me as soon as you know *anything*." They started walking fast, back through the woods in the direction of Becky's car. The last they saw of Vic, he was once again kneeling over Mike Goertz, checking for a pulse.

CHAPTER TWENTY-EIGHT

TIM DIDN'T KNOW how long he had been in the boat. After about ten minutes his legs were tired from kicking the bottom, but kicking made noise that someone might hear, so he started in again. He found he could turn over on his back and lift his bound legs high enough to make a very loud sound when they hit the boat's bottom. He guessed he'd been in the boat maybe an hour when he decided to take another rest, but no sooner had he stopped kicking than he heard a car somewhere close by. He tried to yell, but the cloth over his face muffled his voice. He couldn't get the cloth off, although he had tried by pushing his face against one of the seats and twisting. So he went back to kicking as hard as he could.

Almost immediately, he heard a loud "crack". A few seconds after that, he saw water seeping into the boat right under his feet. He realized he'd kicked a hole in the boat. For a second, this seemed great—maybe he could get out of the boat now. He was a good swimmer. Then he realized that with his hands and feet tied up, he couldn't go anywhere. *I'll drown!* he thought, panicking. *Dad, you have to find me! Dad, you have to come and get me!*

The boat sank slowly. The small hole let just a trickle of water in, but in a few minutes an inch of water filled the bottom of the boat. Mike Goertz had not spent much time with the lines, but he had made sure they were tied to the dock at both the prow and the stern. The lines were long and stout. This meant the boat could sink a few feet. The water level in the lake was high for the time of year. The water seeping into the boat might be enough to drown the young boy lying helplessly in it. Unless someone found him first.

CHAPTER TWENTY-NINE

Jay and Becky piled into Becky's car, and she fumbled for her key. "Are you okay?" Jay asked her anxiously. "Were you getting sick back there? Can you drive?"

Becky reached into the pocket of her pants and pulled out a dirty white tissue. She put it carefully on the console of the car and opened it. Jay saw what looked like dirt inside it.

"Yeah, I've just never seen anyone shot before. I lost my lunch and felt like I was going to faint. But when I was bending over, I had a thought. I picked some dirt out of his tires. This is it. Maybe it's nothing, but maybe it could tell us something about where he drove that car recently—like, maybe, where he drove it to hide Tim."

Jay felt stunned. He slowly reached for the tissue. "Why didn't you tell Vic what you thought?"

Becky paused. "He's kind of an asshole. I don't like him. Let him do his thing. We can do ours."

Jay looked closely at the dirt in the tissue. He had the sensation of time slipping away and his head hurt now, but he concentrated. The dirt looked sandy and red.

"I've been out on Lake Charles lots of times. Most of the side roads and roads near the beaches have dirt like this." He looked at Becky, who was watching him intently.

"How far is it around the whole lake?"

"Not sure—maybe fifteen miles. We're gonna have to go down every side road, look for boat sheds or something like that. Maybe cabins. My guess is he hid Tim somewhere around here." Becky was starting her car as Jay said this. Without answering him, she pulled out of the woods and onto the road leading away from the pumping station. Almost as an after-thought, Jay added, "I think this is the only paved road on the lake, so he didn't get the dirt coming in here."

"Two of his tires were flat," she answered. "Is there any construction around here? He might have picked up nails at a construction site."

Jay recalled fishing on Lake Charles last spring and taking the children to a small beach last summer. But he didn't remember any construction. Now he wished he had paid more attention. "I don't know. Let's just drive down every road we come to, even if it looks like a path. He wouldn't have picked any place too obvious."

They drove until Jay yelled, "There! Turn!" Just ahead and on the right Becky now saw through the trees what looked like two ruts.

She braked and turned. "Do you know where this goes?"

"No, but it looks hidden. Maybe he thought no one else could find it."

The car lurched ahead, but in a few yards they came up to a large fallen oak tree, rotting and dead for some time.

"Bad choice," Jay mumbled as Becky began backing the car down the path. It was too narrow to turn the car around. Just before she got to the main road, she accidentally hit the horn. It gave one raucous blast. Jay jumped as if someone had goosed him. But, to her surprise, Jay leaned over her and hit the horn again.

"That's it!" he yelled, and Becky pulled over and stopped the car.

"What's 'it'? What do you mean?"

"If Tim's anywhere around here, I can try signaling him in Morse code. He may be able to yell back or something."

"But you said the lake is fifteen miles around. Will he hear you?"

"We'll still have to drive down every road, but there aren't many of them. I'll bet he'll find a way to make noise if he hears us!"

Becky stared at him. "You know Morse code? I thought people didn't use that anymore."

"Tim's been studying it for scouts, and I remember enough letters that we can try with the horn."

Becky accelerated and saw the next side road, which at least looked like it was more than two ruts. She turned and drove fast, bouncing the car and finally coming to a dead end where there were two shacks, a dilapidated dock, and no signs of people. "Put the windows down!" Jay yelled and reached over her to blow "TIM ANSWER" in Morse code on the horn.

They waited. Nothing. No signal back.

"Try the next road," Jay said, but she was already turning around. The windows stayed down.

They drove down two more roads in the next eight minutes and tried the signal but got no response. Becky stole a look at Jay after they turned back from the second road. Color was draining from his face. "Do you want to try something else?" she asked softly.

"No! Go to the next road. Hurry." He figured that they less than an hour until darkness.

Half a mile further, the next side road appeared. It had a barrier up at the entrance. It was just a piece of wood, supported on both ends by sawhorses. It had crudely painted letters that read "Private property. Do Not Enter". Becky slowed the car. "What do you want to do?"

Without answering, Jay jumped out of the car and kicked the barrier down. He got back in and sounded the horn with the same Morse code: "TIM ANSWER." Becky started driving slowly down the dirt path. In another minute Jay sounded the horn code again, and she stopped in case the sound of the engine was drowning out a response. Nothing. Nothing— and then, a faint sound.

"Don't drive—listen!" Jay pleaded and sounded the code again. This time, they both heard the sound that came after the horn was silent. It sounded like somebody hitting on something—three short sounds, three with longer spaces between them, and then three short-spaced, but the sounds were faint.

"That's an SOS!" Jay yelled. "Keep driving!" Becky got the car going as fast as she could on the uneven road. They reached the end quickly and saw—nothing, other than a weedy beach. No house, no dock, nothing.

Jay jumped out of the car and then reached back in to sound the horn with the Morse code message one more time. This time, they heard nothing coming back. Becky scrambled out and ran to the water where Jay was already looking frantically around. She saw it first.

"There! Down the beach! There's a dock and a boat. Run!" She took off, not waiting for Jay.

He caught up with her as they covered the fifty yards in what seemed like seconds. He saw a dock in front of a shack. He also saw an open boat tied to the dock. The boat was almost under water. And something was in the boat, not moving.

"Tim! Tim!" Jay's voice grew higher in pitch. Becky kept up with him. They reached the dock. Jay seemed to fly toward the boat. "He's here— help me!"

Becky saw the inert body and the water nearly at the gunwales of the boat. Jay was kneeling on the dock, trying to lift the boy out. Becky knelt to help him. Tim's hands and feet were bound. His head was partly submerged. His eyes were closed. It was hard to tell if he was breathing. But he had signaled them, hadn't he? Hadn't he?

On the dock, Jay performed artificial respiration on Tim. Becky used her cell phone to call 911. There was no response from Tim. Then, suddenly, water came spurting out of his lungs, and they heard a whimper. Jay thought it was the best sound he had ever heard as he kept on pumping Tim's chest. Tears ran down Jay's cheeks. "Tim, Tim—I'm here. I'm here. You're all right."

Tim's eyes fluttered and then stayed open. He was coughing now, and Jay was frantically trying to cut the ropes binding Tim's hands and feet. "They're sending an ambulance," Becky said, bending over to squeeze one of Tim's hands. "Hi, Tim! I'm Becky."

Tim looked at her and then back at his father. He tried to smile. "I wasn't scared. I heard your Morse code! I banged on the sides with my feet."

Jay felt overwhelming relief, but the lump in his throat had grown so much he couldn't say anything. Tim looked around and then, his voice a little stronger, asked both of them, "Where's Colley? Is he okay?"

Jay smiled at his son. "Yes, Tim, he's fine. He escaped. He's home. And that's where you're going, too."

Now Tim's smile was broad. "Dad, the code for 'W' is one short and two long—you forgot the second long. But I knew it was you."

CHAPTER THIRTY

BY THE TIME the ambulance arrived, Jay had carried Tim to Becky's car and laid him on the back seat. They agreed that Jay should ride in the ambulance with Tim, and Becky would drive behind them. Then, they saw the sheriff's car pull in behind the ambulance, and Vic got out. He smiled broadly at both of them and went over to Tim, who was being loaded onto the ambulance stretcher.

"Hey, young man—you had us worried, but your dad found you!" He patted Tim on the head. "We got the bad guy, and your little friend Colley was found. You're gonna be fine, too." Tim gave him a weak smile. Jay knew that Tim always felt a little intimated by Vic.

"My dad and I used Morse code. That's how he found me." Tim sounded proud. This was becoming an adventure now.

The ride to the hospital took twenty minutes, during which time Jay called Emma to tell her Tim was all right. She agreed to meet them in the emergency room. When they got there, Emma was waiting. She was alone. She gave Jay a quick embrace and then bent over the stretcher and gave Tim a long kiss.

"Where's Lynn?" Jay whispered to her.

Emma looked down. "Patrick's home with her."

Just then, Jay saw Becky parking near the entrance. He realized for the first time that Emma knew nothing about Becky. He waited until Becky made it to the door of the emergency room as they were all entering behind the stretcher.

"Emma, this is a friend from work, Becky Franz. She helped me drive to find Tim."

Emma gave Becky a long, level look and then refocused on Jay, who looked very pale and whose arm was still heavily bandaged. "Thank you," she said to Becky, and then she turned to go into the emergency room.

"Maybe I should leave?" Becky asked Jay, hanging back. He hesitated. This felt like more than he could deal with right now, but without Becky, he and Tim would not be here. "No. Come in with us. It's fine." He saw Becky raise an eyebrow, but she followed him in.

The doctors wanted to hold Tim overnight and do some tests, especially after they found the large lump on his head sustained when Mike hit him to the floor. Emma insisted she would stay, but Jay urged her to go home and let Lynn know her brother was all right. Emma gave Tim a long hug and told him she would see him in the morning when he came home. Becky hung back near the admitting desk. Jay realized that he ached in several places and was extremely tired but also elated. Vic stayed with them and got coffee for everybody. Finally, he and Jay had a few minutes alone.

"Is he dead?" Jay asked his brother-in-law, knowing that Vic would know who "he" was.

"Yeah. I thought he had a pulse, but they couldn't revive him. Didn't know I was such a good shot. I'd of liked to see him prosecuted, so I'm sorry about that, but not about his being dead after all he put the boys through."

"Do you think anybody else was in on it?" This was a question that had been bothering Jay for some time, because if the answer was "yes," then they still had to find the accomplice.

Vic paused for a moment. "Doesn't look like it, but we don't know. I'm interviewing Sid Hartman tomorrow. Already talked to him on the phone, and by the way, I called him a few minutes ago to tell him we rescued Tim. I have my men searching Mike's house. They'll come up with something if there's anything to come up with. I confiscated his cell phone, and we'll be checking that, too."

"Where'd you get the money to put in that sack he picked up?"

Vic chuckled. "Always helps to be friends with the president of the biggest bank in the county. Had to give him my personal word we would recover all of it. And, of course, we did. You don't owe me a thing."

This last remark sounded ambiguous to Jay, but he let it go. "I'm going to stay here with Tim. Maybe you could give me a ride home in the morning? With the van gone, I don't have wheels."

Vic looked at Jay appraisingly. "No, I'll stay. You look bad. Let your girlfriend drive you home. You can come back early in the morning. I'd like to talk to Tim—he may be able to remember something if there was anybody else involved."

Jay did not want to leave Tim, but he knew his own stamina was fading. "Thanks. Call me if anything happens tonight, like if he starts to run a fever, or calls out for me, or anything."

Vic squeezed Jay's good arm. "I will. Get some rest."

Jay went into the small, private room where they had moved Tim, whose eyes were closed. They had given him a light sedative. Jay bent over the bed and held his son for a few seconds. "Tim," he whispered, "I could never have been as brave as you were. I'm so proud of you. I have to go home and get some sleep now, but your uncle Vic will be here all night with you. And your mother and I will be back in the morning." Tim opened his eyes and smiled sleepily at his father. "Okay. Thanks, Dad. Thanks for finding me—and Becky, too. I love you."

Jay found Becky by the admitting desk and told her what was happening. "I'd rather stay, but I guess I need some rest," he told her, and she nodded. "Let's go."

As they walked out into the starry evening, Jay could see Becky giving him a sidelong glance. He wondered what she was thinking. Maybe she liked him even better after they worked together to rescue his son?

CHAPTER THIRTY-ONE

V IC TIPTOED INTO Tim's hospital room and listened to Tim's light breathing. He wondered if Tim would wake up long enough for some questions but decided he shouldn't push it. Belatedly, he remembered that he had promised to stop over at Louise's for a beer or whatever later that evening. He stepped outside Tim's room to call her.

"I understand, Vic. We'll make up for it later. Maybe I'll see you in the morning there. I'll come by Tim's room and we can have coffee downstairs. I was going visit my next door neighbor in the hospital anyway—she's just had a new knee put in."

"Sounds good. Thanks, Lou. Maybe we can catch that new sci-fi flick at the Twin Hills next week." One of the things Vic liked about Louise was her independence, but he also liked the fact that they had a good time together.

Tim was awake when Vic went back into the room. "Uncle Vic, what time is it?"

Vic looked at the lighted dial on his watch. "Few minutes after nine. You need water or anything?" Tim nodded and Vic poured water from the pitcher into the glass on the side table near the bed. "Anything else?"

"Yeah, I'm kinda hungry. Do you think they'd let me have anything?"

"I'll go ask at the desk. You sit tight." Tim smiled at him as he finished his water.

Fifteen minutes later, Vic arrived back with a large hamburger and French fries, wrapped in paper. "Best fast food the cafeteria could offer." He sat down across from Tim's bed and watched the boy eagerly unwrap his food.

Vic waited a few minutes until Tim laid the second half of the sandwich down on the paper and then said, "Tim, the man who kidnapped you and Colley was named Mike. When you were with him, did you ever hear him make any phone calls to anyone or talk about anybody?"

Tim thought hard. Some of the time he knew he had been unconscious. But he didn't remember hearing the man—Mike—talking to anyone on his phone. "I think he made a call after he got me out of the basement, after he hit me. He thought I was out cold but I can kind of remember.

He had me in his car, and he got out to make a phone call. I didn't hear it, though." Tim's voice trailed off.

"Suppose you tell me everything you remember, from after you and your dad rescued Colley in that old house?"

Tim was wide awake now, and he clearly wanted to talk about his adventure, so he gave Vic all the details he could think of. When he finished, Vic walked over to the bed and gave him a hug. "This will be very helpful, Tim. You have a good memory. You would make a good witness in court. Unfortunately, we've got one bad guy dead and nobody else."

Tim's eyes widened. "You mean Mike is *dead*? What happened?"

"I had to shoot him. He shot at me first, right after he got the ransom money. I didn't want him to end up dead, either, but it happened. Your dad and his friend were there, too, and I didn't want them to get hurt."

Just then, the night nurse came in to check on him, and eventually, Tim drifted back to sleep. Vic stayed with him and dosed off and on.

When the sunlight filtered through the blinds, it was 6 a.m. Vic's phone was vibrating. He went out into the hallway. "Yeah?"

"Vic, it's me, Jay. I'm coming down to the hospital now. My landlord's driving me, and Emma's going to meet me after the sitter comes for Lynn. How is Tim?"

"Seems fine. He's still asleep. He ate a whole burger and fries last night, and we had a good talk. He told me as much as he could remember about what happened after you crashed the van, but he doesn't remember anything about an accomplice."

"I'm on my way."

§ § §

When Alex Rosen let Jay out in front of the hospital, Jay saw Vic's friend Louise parking her car in the lot. He waited for her.

"Hey, Louise. What brings you here?" He smiled at her—everyone in town liked Louise.

"Jay! I talked with Vic last night and know all about Timmy and that other little boy. I'm so glad Timmy is all right. You look a little banged up though. How are you?"

"Much better now that we have Tim back. Wouldn't have happened without Vic. He's been great through all this." Jay held the door for her and they headed for the elevator.

"Vic takes his work very seriously. You know that, Jay. I respect that, even if it means we haven't had an evening together for the last two months—but I can wait! He's doing a lot of good for this community. And he did say I could buy him coffee this morning. I'll follow you to Tim's room. I told him I'd meet him there."

Tim was sitting on the edge of the bed when they walked in. He jumped us, still wearing his hospital gown, and ran to hug Jay. Vic struggled to his feet. His eyes were bloodshot, and he looked like he had spent the night in an uncomfortable chair, which he had.

"Hello, Lou!" he said with enthusiasm.

Tim smiled shyly at her. "Hello, Miss Louise." She stepped around Jay to give Tim a vigorous hug.

"Dad, I want to get out of here! All they brought me for breakfast was some yucky oatmeal. Can we go to the Waffle House? Please?"

"Tim, we'll go anywhere you want, but first the doctors have to check you out. Your mom is on her way here."

At that moment, Emma peered around the door. "Can I join the party?"

Tim ran to her and hugged her around her knees. "Mom! Did you bring Lynn? Dad says we can go out to breakfast! And Uncle Vic told me he shot the man who kidnapped me and Colley. Did you know that?"

Emma smiled broadly but tears came to her eyes. "Lynn's waiting for us at home with Arlene. And I know how Uncle Vic helped you. I think the doctors want to have one last look at you." She turned to Vic. "Thank you for spending the night. Thank you for everything."

"I didn't do much," Vic said, looking down at the floor. Then he took Louise by the arm. "Come on. You said we could have coffee. I could use some." He turned to Jay and Emma. "If you need anything, I'm going back to the office after I leave here. I've got a report to file and some work to do. I'll let you know if we find out anything. Goodbye, Tim. Thanks for talking with me last night. I'm proud of you." He gave them all a small smile and ushered Louise out the door. She turned and waved as they left.

Jay smiled at both of them, even as he felt a tingling at the back of his brain. There was something he needed to ask Vic, something that might be important—but what? *Oh, well, it will come to me later*, he told himself, just as the on-duty doctor entered the room with a hearty "Good morning! How are you today, Tim? Let's see if we can get you out of here!"

CHAPTER THIRTY-TWO

A FTER THE HOSPITAL released Tim, Jay and Emma agreed to pick up Lynn and invite Arlene to go with all of them to the Waffle House. Then, Emma would take them home, and Jay promised to come over for dinner. Jay did not ask about Patrick, and Emma made no mention of Becky. *Just one big happy family*, he thought later, paying the bill for breakfast and looking at the smiles around the table. But he knew it wasn't true.

After Emma dropped him off at his apartment, Jay called his foreman, Carlos, to explain what had been happening and to ask a favor. "Carlos, have you still got that old Dodge RAM for sale? I need wheels, and I'll pay you to rent it to me until I can get something else."

Carlos quickly agreed to let Jay use the Dodge, free of charge, and promised to bring it over within the hour. His wife would follow him and drive him home. The prospect of having the truck along with knowing Tim was all right made Jay feel good enough that he almost forgot his occasional aches. He had one more very important thing to do this morning. He dialed Becky.

"Hey, I was kinda out of it last night when you dropped me off. There's no way I can thank you for helping me find Tim." He wanted to say a couple of other things but suddenly found he didn't have the right words.

"That's all right. Did they release Tim? How is he feeling?"

"Yeah, he's good, and he's home now."

"Great!" There was a pause, then, "If you don't have lunch plans, I could pick up some subs and cokes and come over."

Jay thought quickly. Carlos would be bringing the Dodge over but would leave right after that. "Sounds good! All I've got here are a couple of apples and beer."

"I'll be there around 2."

After Carlos delivered the truck, Jay straightened up the apartment. He also called Alex to say he would be available the following weekend for more apple picking or anything else Alex needed done. He made a quick call to Sid to fill him in on Tim's rescue and listened while Sid shared that he and Deb had a long talk and were thinking about reconciling "for Colley's sake." Jay wondered privately if the law wouldn't come after Deb for her part in letting Mike take her son. Jay promised Sid he would contact him so they could have a beer or two in a few days.

He showered for the second time that day, keeping his bandages away from the shower spray as best he could, and then dressed in clean jeans and a sport shirt. His hair, as usual, refused to lie down in one direction so he gave up on it.

When he heard the knock on his apartment door, he was ready. He opened it and stepped back to admire his visitor. Becky's peasant skirt in blue and white reached almost to her ankles. Her white, ruffled, off-the-shoulder blouse complemented her smooth, tan skin. A fragrance wafted in—he couldn't identify it, but it seemed spicy and nice. He held the door open wide.

"This is your take-out order, sir," Becky said as she brushed past him to lay down a large bag from the sub shop and a six pack of Cokes in his tiny kitchen. She opened her purse and extracted a pint of dark rum. "Thought this might go well with the Cokes," she said, turning to him and smiling.

"Do you want some now?" Jay asked, still looking at her and thinking that she seemed so much softer, so much more feminine than he had previously noticed.

"Sure, but just one—I'm driving!"

He mixed the drinks, and Becky laid out the sandwiches on the TV tray across from the television and in front of the couch. "I saw an old Dodge RAM out front. Is that your new wheels?"

"Courtesy of Carlos. He's letting me use it until they fix the van."

"He seems like a good guy. I like working on his detail." Becky sat down and accepted the glass Jay handed her. "Here—have something to eat. I went to a lot of trouble to fix these!"

They both laughed, and instead of talking about Tim and all that had happened, Becky wanted to know about Alex Rosen and the orchard. Jay described how they cultivated the apples and were now close to the harvesting stage. When they had finished eating, he took the remains of their lunch to the sink and came back to sit next to her.

"I really can't thank you enough for all you've done. Tim knows it, too." He took both of her hands in his and held them for a minute.

Becky looked down. "It wasn't all that much. Glad I was around."

They were both silent for a minute. Then Jay asked a question that he felt was safe. "You told me that first night we sat in the van that you want to finish at the college and maybe stay here. What would you do?"

Instead of answering right away, Becky withdrew her hands and got up to look out the window at the orchard. "I'm not sure. Depends on some things. Depends on whether I'm single—or not. But I want to make some good money. Ben's big on money, too. I never felt like we had enough when I was growing up, although my dad's Army salary was not bad. But I want nice things. And I'm willing to work hard to get them. I'm good with numbers, but I'm also good with my hands fixing things, even building things. That's why I took the construction job—good pay, outdoors, operating equipment. Maybe I'll start my own business someday. I could do car repair. 'Course, there seems to be enough of those businesses around here."

She turned back to him. "What about you? I don't see you working construction forever."

Jay sighed. He didn't really want to have a serious conversation right now, but he had started it. He got up to stand next to her. She moved close to him, and he put an arm around her waist.

"I have a fantasy about starting a new life, but I think it's just that—a fantasy. I could join my folks at their nursery. If I had more money, I might buy into Alex's business and help him expand. He's offered, but I can't even think about that until I'm sure about what's going to happen with Emma and the kids. Sometimes, it's kind of depressing."

To his surprise and without another word, Becky reached up to his face with both hands and drew his head down to hers. She kissed him gently and then harder on the mouth, letting him taste the faint scent of the rum and Coke and also her perfume. They held the embrace for a long time, and then Jay took her hand and led her back to the couch. It was an old brown leather couch and wide. A blanket lay across the back. Jay put the blanket on the seat, picked Becky up and laid her on the blanket. He covered her body with his and waited for her to open her mouth again, which she did quickly and urgently.

He wasn't thinking now, just letting his instincts and his desire dictate what would happen. He pushed down the front edge of her blouse. She was not wearing anything under it. Her well-shaped breasts were warm to his touch, her nipples hard. He moved his mouth to her right breast and she moaned softly. He felt her hand between his legs. When she began to unzip his jeans, he did not resist. This was going to be what he dreamed about and wanted.

And then, suddenly, he knew he could not go on. He was going to see his family—his real family—in just a few hours. He had a wife, although he didn't know if she still wanted him. But at this moment, he knew that as much as he wanted Becky, as beautiful as she was to him, he couldn't act on it—not yet. He gently moved her hand away from him, pulled her blouse back up and knelt down in front of the couch.

"Becky, I can't do this right now. I'm so sorry. I've thought about doing this for days, but I can't. I have to see Tim tonight, and there's too much I have to sort out. Can you, please, understand that? I do want you."

She stared at him for a moment, and then, to his surprise, burst out laughing. "Well, gee, I guess I know a brush off when I get one!" She reached out for his hand and squeezed it. "Yeah, I think I understand. Maybe it's too quick for us. But I like you. I wanted you to ask me here and for us to be like this. I hope this isn't goodbye."

"I promise it isn't. You can count on that. It's just that I'm trying to sort things out."

"And you have something to do tonight, so I'm going to leave." She stood up, smoothed out her skirt, and ran a hand through her hair. Jay admired her composure.

"Let me walk you out to your car." He went in the kitchen and put the small bottle of rum back in its bag. "You can take this home and serve me one some time."

"Does that mean we're going to see each other again?"

"I've already said yes, but yes."

They walked to her car in silence, but when they got there Jay took her in his arms and gave her another long kiss. He didn't care if anybody was watching. "Thank you for lunch—and everything."

She got in the car, lowered the window, and gave him a little wave. "See you at work!"

§ § §

Late that afternoon, Mike's accomplice was doing some serious thinking. "Let's see: both boys rescued, no ransom, Mike dead." The information had been all over the local TV news. "Is there anyone who can identify me? Not likely. That boy doesn't know anything much, but, of course, I can't be sure how careless Mike was. He acted without thinking things through sometimes." Maybe it was best to chalk this one up as a failure and move on? Was there any other choice? *Was* Tim still a risk? And if he was, what to do about him? There was an instinct to eliminate trouble. "Maybe I should follow my instincts."

116

CHAPTER THIRTY-THREE

SOMETIME AFTER BECKY left, Jay went out to the orchard. He needed to walk and think. *How can I make this come out right?* he asked himself over and over again. He felt it was likely that he and Emma were through, *but maybe there's a chance we can work things out?* Part of the problem, he realized, was that he didn't exactly know what those "things" were or if he even wanted to try. And now, there was Becky. He had tried not to be attracted to her, but after the events of the past week he knew his feelings for her went deeper than gratitude. *And I don't know how she really feels about Ben.* They never seemed to talk about Ben.

This set him off on a different path. *What if I got a divorce and Becky broke up with Ben? I've got to stay here for the kids; I can't leave them. Would Becky stay here, too?* She told him she wanted to finish college, and she was ambitious, especially about money. Maybe it wouldn't work out and then he'd be on his own again. Or was all this about his just not wanting to be alone?

Without realizing it, he had walked through the entire orchard and now turned around to hurry back to get ready to join Emma and the children for dinner. For some reason, it now seemed urgent to him to get to the house early and to be sure Tim was all right. He knew that everything was all right now with Tim, but he still wanted to see his son more than ever.

Jay kept thinking about the last twenty-four hours. Fragments of conversations came back to him in no particular order. He remembered vividly the relief he felt finding Tim in that boat, alive. He remembered coming back to the hospital this morning and finding Tim in good shape. He remembered the feeling of Becky's body beneath him and the scent of her freshly washed hair.

And then, for no apparent reason, he remembered his parking lot conversation with Louise. Suddenly, the tingling in the back of his mind started up again as he heard her voice saying, "even if it means we haven't had an evening together for the last two months." She had been talking about how busy Vic was.

But hadn't Vic told Jay and Emma that he was with Louise on Friday night, the night of the accident, and that was why he had his phone turned off? Jay tried to remember Vic's exact words: something about having been to dinner with Louise and then going back to her place.

Jay got out of the shower dripping wet and stood still on the bathroom rug. He wondered why Vic would lie about something like this, unless Vic just wanted everybody to think he and Louise had a hot thing going. Jay felt bewildered. Would telling that lie really be on Vic's mind when his own nephew was missing? Or had Vic been someplace else that he didn't want Jay to know about? Maybe Vic had actually been doing some surveillance himself and didn't want anybody to know. But then why wouldn't Vic simply have told Jay that?

It didn't add up. Should he call Louise and ask her about that evening? No, because it was possible Vic had been with another woman. Jay didn't want to get Vic in trouble. Maybe Louise's comment was just an exaggeration. Maybe they had been together and she was just making a point that they hadn't seen much of each other recently. The more Jay thought about it, the more likely this last explanation seemed. He knew people did exaggerate for very personal reasons. He could ask Vic about that night later, just to resolve the issue. He decided to do that on Monday after work.

The evening with Emma and the kids felt like an anticlimax. The adults were tired. Tim wanted to tell his story over and over again. They listened patiently, but it was a strain for both parents to hear the details when they knew how easily things could have turned out otherwise. Jay put both children to bed a little later than usual and then said to Emma, "We need to talk."

He did not want to alarm her, but he had to tell her there was a chance that Mike had an accomplice and that whoever that was—if there was anyone—could still come after Tim. "I'm going to go to the sheriff's tomorrow," Jay added, not telling Emma that he also had a specific question to ask Vic. "I'll ask them to send a cruiser by here regularly. In the meantime, you have my .22. You know it's loaded. I know you keep it locked up in the closet upstairs, but don't be afraid to get it out if anyone suspicious comes around. And keep your cell phone on—I'll do the same."

Emma listened without commenting and then said, "Do you really think we are in danger?"

"No, I don't, but I just wanted you to know that there is this one loose end. I'm sure the sheriff's people will clear it up. And there may not be anything to it."

Jay thought that maybe he should offer to stay at the house—that maybe that's what Emma wanted him to do. But then she said, "I feel safe here. I'll call you if anything happens. You and Vic, too. We'll be all right." She hesitated. "And Patrick's here a lot, too, so we're not alone." Her face, as Jay looked at her, seemed like a mask. In the very recent past, this would have angered and upset him. But after his own afternoon, he didn't know how he felt about Patrick. Better to leave that alone, for now.

"I'm going to work tomorrow," he said, getting up from his chair. "I'll call you when I get home tomorrow night and let you know if I find out anything at the sheriff's. I can take Tim to baseball practice on Tuesday, so I'll see you then." For the first time in weeks, he bent over and kissed her lightly on the cheek. She looked surprised but simply said, "thank you." Jay couldn't tell if that was meant for his reassurances or for the kiss.

CHAPTER THIRTY-FOUR

ANOTHER MONDAY PROMISING to get hotter as the day went on. When Jay parked the Dodge, he could scarcely believe that exactly one week ago everything had started—seeing Colley's hand at the window, the accident, Tim's kidnapping, all of it. He passed the brick house as he drove in. The scarred front looked ugly. He could see that there were a few charred pieces of wood on the ground and broken glass. The "for sale" sign was still up. He wondered if the property would be worth much now.

Becky pulled into the parking lot a few minutes after him. She was wearing a new pair of jeans and a light blue, long-sleeved cotton work shirt. Jay thought she looked terrific. She smiled at him and came over to give his arm a pat. "Good morning! Did you have a good weekend?"

"In more ways than I could imagine!" Jay replied, grinning at her.

Her look became serious. "How is Tim?"

"He's fine. I tucked them both in last night. I think he's looking forward to telling the whole baseball team about his adventure."

They both left the parking lot. "I'm working on the trencher today. Maybe we can eat lunch together?" She gave him a questioning look.

"I'd like that, and dinner, too."

Becky looked past him a moment. "Well, okay, but I have a few things to do this evening. Can we make it kind of late? Maybe eight o'clock? Do you want me to pick you up?"

"I'll pick you up. You decide where we should go." He felt like this day was starting out just right. He didn't even feel any aches or pains so far.

By the end of the afternoon, however, Jay felt both hot and tired. He still had to visit the sheriff's office. First, he was going to see about getting some extra security for Emma and the kids. Second, he was going to try and find out why Vic had lied about where he was the night of the accident. He drove the seven miles between the work site and the sheriff's office thinking of how he would phrase his question to Vic, but when he got there, the desk clerk informed him "Sheriff Bartle is on assignment." Jay was ready to leave when she added, "Sheriff Carlson is here now if you want to see him."

Jay hadn't seen Chris Carlson for several months. Chris, a one-time football player now 62, was fit and tanned. He got up immediately to shake Jay's hand and join him on the other side of the desk. "Jay—good to see you." He motioned to a chair and they both sat down.

"I'm so sorry about your boy—about the whole thing. Sorry, too, that I was away when most of this happened. I've read all the reports, and Vic's filled me in on everything. We have a background check on Mike Goertz. We already know he had some minor brushes with the law over the last ten years, but nothing like kidnapping. There was some evidence he might have been involved in that drug ring we broke up a few years ago, but not enough proof to charge him with anything. My men haven't found anything important at his apartment, but we'll keep digging. We're interviewing his family, his girlfriend, Deborah Hartman, and everybody where he worked. Is there anything you want to tell us, or has Tim remembered anything more? I know Vic had a long talk with him in the hospital."

"Tim's fine, but he hasn't said anything more than what I guess you know. I'm just worried that if Mike had an accomplice that guy might be afraid of what Tim knows—even though he doesn't know anything. So, I was wondering if you could have your men drive by my house—Emma's house—on a regular basis for a few days. At least until you're positive there's nobody else involved."

"Of course. We'll keep it up for a couple of weeks and see where we are. Does Emma have any guns at the house?"

"Yes, she has my .22. It's loaded and locked away from the kids. She knows how to use it." Jay thought of something else. "Vic said you got Mike's cell phone. Anything on that you could use?"

"No, unfortunately. Everything was erased. There were two other phones in the glove compartment of his car, but they were pay-as-you-go ones with nothing useful on them either. He probably erased everything before he went for the ransom. But, Jay, he wasn't all that smart—he made mistakes. So, if someone was helping him, we'll find him."

"I guess you've got Vic out on assignment. Is he out of town? I had a couple of things I wanted to ask him."

"I told him to take a couple of days off. Technically, the State Police have to investigate the shooting. Shouldn't be any problem. It was clearly self-defense."

Jay was thinking about something else Chris Carlson had said. "When was that drug bust you mentioned? I sort of remember it, but I don't remember hearing anything about Mike Goertz being involved."

"It was just over four years ago this month, and I don't think Mike's name ever got in the papers. We had nothing concrete on him, and we don't give out names until after we've charged people. There was an awful lot of confusing publicity about it anyway. Vic had a lot to do with solving the case, and he kept the lid on lots of stuff we didn't want to get out. We caught the ring that was responsible, and they'd been dealing in this county for over three years. They're all behind bars now."

Jay stood up and reached out to shake the sheriff's hand. "Chris, thanks for seeing me. And thanks for setting up a patrol. I know Emma will feel much better, and I do, too. If Tim says anything to us that sounds like you should hear it, I'll let you or Vic know."

"And I'll get back to you if we find out anything more about anybody Goertz might have been working with."

Jay let himself out, with a nod to the desk clerk. Should he go home now and get ready for his dinner date, or should he try and find Vic? It was only 5:30 p.m. Then he had another idea: he would visit Louise.

CHAPTER THIRTY-FIVE

L OUISE WAGNER LIVED in an old farmhouse and operated her potter's shed in what had once been the barn. Jay tried her door-bell first, but when no one came, he walked around to the shed. The door was open, and he could see Louise, her hair bound up in a red scarf, cleaning one of her potter's wheels.

She turned just as he entered. "Jay! What a nice surprise! Don't tell me you're shopping this time of day." Two years ago, Jay bought one of her vases for Emma, who put it in the center of their dining room table. Even Jay could see that Louise's work was very fine.

"No, not shopping, but I was driving by so I thought I would come and see you."

"Well, come on in. I'm just cleaning up. How's Tim?"

"Doing well, thanks. He'll be back to playing baseball this week, I think." Jay paused. He was not sure how to go on.

Louise cocked her head. "What's on your mind?"

She was sitting in her potter's chair, and Jay sat down on the high stool across from her. "Louise, I feel funny asking you, this but it's bothering me. The other night, after my accident with the van when the boys got taken, well, later at the hospital Emma tried to call Vic. She couldn't get him at home or on his cell. Then he came in later and said he was at dinner with you and took you home and had his phone turned off. But you said the other day that you and Vic hadn't been together in quite a while. It's probably none of my business, and maybe I'm being stupid, but some-thing about this is bothering me."

Louise said nothing for a minute. She took off the scarf and shook out her graying curls. She laid the scarf down on her lap and finally looked up at Jay. "I don't know the answer, Jay. Vic and I, well, we usually see each other when it's convenient and we both feel like it. But it's been pretty regular up until about three months ago. Now, he doesn't tell me much about what he's doing. And that's all right, but we used to share. I think he's got some-thing going on, but I don't know what. Maybe there's another lady in his life." She said this last thing lightly, but Jay could tell he had hit a nerve.

"Louise, I feel really bad bothering you with this. I'm sure it's nothing. It's just the last few days for me, for us, well, I'm thinking back on everything now. Trying to figure out why all this happened. The kidnapping, the accident, everything."

"You've been through a lot. If I knew what's going on with Vic, I'd tell you, but I don't." Louise looked steadily at Jay. Then, "You don't think he had anything to do with the boys kidnapping, do you?"

Jay felt blood rising to his cheeks. In the last few hours, he had thought about this, and the truth was that he no longer knew what to think. He didn't consider Vic a friend or even a good brother-in-law, but Vic had helped with Tim and that mattered a lot to Jay.

"I don't think he was involved, but he may know something or was doing something—or something," he finished lamely.

"Jay, if I thought for a minute Vic was mixed up in all that's happened, I would tell you—and then I would go to Sheriff Carlson. Vic has his faults, but I've never known him to be dishonest." Louise paused again and this time looked toward the windows of the shed. "But maybe I don't know him as well as I thought."

It was clear to Jay that the conversation would go no further, and he didn't want to hurt her. "Look, Louise, I appreciate your talking with me. I'm still trying to make sense of things. I don't suspect Vic of anything, and if I sounded like it, I didn't mean it. Thank you for being a good friend." He got up.

Louise stood up and took his right hand in both of hers. "No offense taken. I can see you're still in some pain—about a lot of things. If I see or hear of anything that will help, I'll be in touch."

CHAPTER THIRTY-SIX

BACK AT HIS apartment, Jay cleaned up, carefully taking most of his bandages off first. Nothing bled. He took two ibuprofen for the aches he was now feeling and resisted popping a beer. At 7:30, he called Emma to report he had seen Sheriff Carlson since Vic was out for a couple of days. He explained that the sheriff was putting a security detail on their house. Emma thanked him. She told him that Tim played with friends outside most of the day except for a short nap in the afternoon. Jay told her he would come by to pick Tim up for baseball practice the next afternoon at 4:30 and have dinner with them afterwards. He did not tell her his plans for this evening.

At 7:55 p.m., Jay pulled up outside Becky's apartment building. Knowing he was early, he called her. "Hey, I'm down on the street. I know I'm early but I can wait here—or come up."

"Come on! We can have a drink here first. I've still got to clean up."

When Becky opened the door, she was in dirt-streaked jeans with a grease smudge on her right cheek. "Been helping a friend across the street with her car. It's a mess. She's not good with mechanical things, but my dad taught me just about everything to do with cars, at least the older ones. I got it running, too! Sorry about not being ready."

He laughed, delighted just to see her and to get a look at her apartment, which was modest—just two rooms plus a small kitchen and bathroom. Books were piled on top of most surfaces. "Are you up for a drink? Beer or something stronger?" she asked, after giving him a light kiss on the lips. She smelled of diesel fuel.

"A gin and tonic sounds pretty good if you have the makings. Or a beer. Whatever you've got." Jay was feeling relaxed for the first time all day.

"A G and T is manageable, but I don't have any lime. I'll make you the drink and then hop in the shower. Sorry I'm running late."

With his drink in hand, Jay sat on the love seat near the television. He looked around the room. Very few pictures. One framed photo he assumed was of her mother and father. Another showed two small children with an adult woman. None of single males. Maybe she had removed "Ben" for the evening? He didn't really care. He was on his third sip when he heard a sharp "ping" and realized Becky had left her smart phone on the kitchen counter.

He wasn't going to bother her while she was taking her shower to tell her she had a text message, but he found himself getting up and moving toward the kitchen. He stopped a foot away from the counter. He could hear her shower water running full blast. He suddenly had an overwhelming urge to look at the message. He hesitated. He never searched through Emma's emails or online records, but now, all of a sudden, he wanted to know who texted Becky.

He scrolled open to her messages. The text just sent came from an area code he did not recognize. The message simply read "call me". He assumed it was from Ben. For a second, he thought about deleting it, then felt ashamed. He did make a mental note of the number. Then, because he had the phone open, he scrolled back through earlier text messages. There were several of them, some from the same area code number he had just seen but all the others from numbers in their local area. He assumed that Ben texted her regularly. He felt embarrassed and put the phone down carefully where she had left it.

When Becky came out of her bedroom, Jay was watching the sports news roundup on television. "Wow, you clean up good!" he said, appreciatively. The simple black slacks and red blouse complimented her coloring and hair. He had never seen her in high heels, but tonight she had on red sandals that looked expensive and sexy. As she went into the kitchen to make herself a drink, he called after her, "I think you got a text message. Your phone beeped." She picked up the phone and, frowning, opened the message. She smiled. "It's my mom! She wants me to call her. I can do that later."

Jay sat back, surprised. Was the message from her mother? He had memorized the number and could check on the area code later. She had told him her folks lived in South Carolina. Jay thought he remembered that Ben was at Fort Hood, Texas, but had lived in Florida, so he probably had a phone number with either a Florida or Texas area code. Well, he would check those area codes when he could. No big deal, and she probably wouldn't want to mention hearing from Ben right now.

"Where do you want to go?" he asked after she sat down by him with her beer.

"Italian might be nice. How about Migliato's—it's about 15 minutes from here. You been there?"

He told her he had not, and as they drove, she described in some detail

Migliato's menu, which proved to be as extensive as she said. By the time their main courses came—chicken cacciatore for Jay and sea bass with pine nuts for Becky, their conversation had moved from work to Becky's hopes to attend college to Jay's family situation. In thinking about the evening beforehand, Jay knew there were some things he needed to say to Becky, and he figured this was as good a time to say them as any.

"Look, I should tell you that I don't know what's really going to happen with Emma, me, and the kids. It's been hard for me to sort out, and this thing with Tim has made it even harder. I don't want to be away from him, but I'm not sure Emma and I have anything left either." He took a long sip of his red wine. The next part was going to be harder.

"Becky, I loved being with you yesterday, and I'd like to do more. But I just can't until I figure all this out. I'm still married, and I don't want to involve you in anything that might hurt you later." He could see her look of surprise followed by a frown.

"I'm not going to get hurt!"

"I know you're strong, but you've got Ben, and I've got a complicated situation. I promise to figure it out soon. And you need to decide about Ben, too." Her lips tensed, but he couldn't read what she was thinking.

"You let me worry about Ben. He's not here."

This exchange brought the evening to an awkward point, and Jay did not know how to make it any better, so he plowed ahead. "Well, maybe we can just keep seeing each other until we both figure out what we want."

Becky folded her napkin and gave him a half smile. "Sure. Whatever. But don't not do anything because of Ben."

Jay wondered if her change in attitude about Ben was because of Jay himself or something that had come between Becky and Ben. He didn't want to ask.

They stayed for coffee, but the easy mood from earlier in the evening was broken. They made some small talk about the food while Jay paid the bill.

When Jay got to Becky's apartment, he parked the car by the curb and turned off the engine. Becky leaned over and gave him a quick kiss on the cheek. "It's late, and I'm not going to ask you in. I guess we both have things to think about. It was a nice dinner—thank you." She reached for the door handle.

Jay felt let down but not surprised. What had he expected, anyway, after what he had told her? "Good night Becky. I promise to work on my issues. See you in the morning."

He waited until she was inside the building before he drove off. The first thing he did when he got to the apartment was to open his laptop and Google the phone number from her text message. Without much effort, he found out that it was a South Carolina area code. He entered the entire phone number in a search program, but the only information that came up was, not surprisingly, that it was not a land line. Maybe the text really was from her mother? But if so, why no texts from Ben? At least none from Florida or Texas area codes. He wondered if Ben only called her and did not text often, but he doubted this was true. He had seen Becky texting and felt sure Ben responded, and he remembered she said they texted each other often. He felt a tingling sensation that was not unpleasant. But he had no way to know anything for certain about Ben and Becky right now, so he gave up.

He went to bed confused, but with a small glimmer of hope that maybe Becky was available or could be. And right now he was looking forward to taking Tim to baseball practice the next day. *Maybe things will get back to normal*, he thought as he drifted off, but not before he had one more thought, *I wonder what 'normal' is now?*

CHAPTER THIRTY-SEVEN

T HE CAR DROVE by Emma's house just before dawn on Tuesday morning. The driver saw the patrol car parked across the street. There were no lights on in the house, and no sign of life. *If the boy still likes to run in the morning, I can wait*, the driver thought. But after a few minutes there was no sign of Tim. Maybe this wasn't the best idea? The car drove slowly to the end of the block and then sped off. It was time to think of something else to be done about Tim.

§ § §

Jay's day began with a text from Becky. It read: "Got a touch of the flu. Hope you don't. Will call later." Since he felt fine and was enjoying a two egg McMuffin breakfast at McDonald's, he wrote her back: "Sorry. Fine here. Taking Tim to practice later. Get well." He thought about her several times during the morning, but he had to concentrate on the traffic, which was heavier than usual, and his mind went to other things, especially to Tim and Emma. Finally, quitting time came and Jay checked out. He thought about calling Becky but decided to wait until later, maybe during Tim's baseball practice.

He arrived at the house a few minutes after 4:00 p.m. Emma saw him and came out on the porch, giving him a little wave. He smiled as he walked up the steps. At least they could be pleasant to each other.

"He's all ready to go," Emma said, pointing inside to the kitchen where Tim was grabbing cookies for the road. "If you want to take him out for supper after practice, that's fine. Lynn and I can manage on our own."

"Hi, Dad!" Tim ran to Jay and hugged him. "Got us some cookies!"

"Thanks, sport. We need to hit the road."

They rode in silence for a few minutes. Tim finished his second cookie. Without looking directly at his father, he asked in a quiet voice, "Dad, are you seeing Becky?"

Jay didn't know what prompted the question, and he thought that anything he said might get back to Emma, but he didn't want to lie to his son. "Yes, I do see her. We work together." He glanced at Tim and was delighted to see Tim smiling.

"Good! I like her." The conversation ended there.

As they drove, Jay noticed a few dark clouds moving along the western sky. He knew how much Tim was looking forward to practice and hoped that the rain, if any, would hold off. A few minutes away from the ball field, Jay glanced in his rear view mirror and thought he saw one of the sheriff's cars staying a few car lengths behind them. He felt reassured that Sheriff Carlson was taking the surveillance seriously.

When they got to the ball field, Tim ran over to the shelter where most of his teammates were milling around, waiting for the coach to get them started. Jay parked the truck and got out. He planned to sit in the stands for the whole practice, which could last up to two hours, and then take Tim out for hamburgers or pizza—whatever he wanted. He walked over to the bleachers and joined some of the other parents who already were seated. One of the younger moms—Jay thought she looked about sixteen with her pony tail— smiled at him. "We're all glad Tim's safe!" she said, squeezing Jay's hand.

He wished he could remember her name, but he smiled back. "Thank you—so are we."

"Okay, men, red squad on the field!" The coach blew his whistle. Tim was playing "red" today, so he would be in the field, with the "blues" at the plate. Then they would switch. Tim was playing third base, as usual. The first ten minutes didn't look good for the "reds," as the other squad rapidly scored two runs and then got the bases loaded with no outs. But the second "reds" pitcher, a small boy with a steady arm, struck out the next boy up, and the second baseman caught a high fly ball from the next batter. Jay looked forward to seeing Tim at the plate. At that moment, his phone rang. It was Becky.

"Jay. I hope this isn't a bad time. Are you at Tim's practice?" Her voice sounded a bit muffled, even weak.

"I am, but that's all right. I was going to call you. How are you feeling?" Jay moved out of the bleachers to take the call and was standing under them.

"Well, that's partly why I'm calling. I'm not good. I've really got something, and I don't know what it is. I'm spending most of my time in the bathroom. I can't seem to hold down any food or even water. I'm throwing up about every half hour. I don't think I can make it to the Medicine Shoppe, so I'm calling to ask a big favor. Could you get a refill of a prescription I have there? I've had something like this before, and I have one refill left. And maybe I could use some Imodium, too."

132

Jay thought rapidly. He didn't want to ask Becky to wait two hours for him to get there, which was about what it might take if he waited until the end of Tim's practice and then had to detour to the Medicine Shoppe. But he didn't want to leave Tim, either. He glanced out at the road. No sign of the sheriff's car now, but a deputy might be close by. And, besides, he could ask one of the other parents to watch out for Tim and even take him home if Jay didn't get back by the end of practice.

"I can be there in about fifteen minutes if your pills are ready for me to pick up. Is that soon enough? Or do you think you should maybe go to the hospital? You could call for an ambulance."

There was a short pause. "I don't want to go to the hospital. I don't have any insurance, and I'm sure the pills and the Imodium will take care of it, but if you can't come, I'll try to find someone else." Jay thought she sounded close to tears.

"I'm coming! I just need to let Tim know that I'll be away for a little while. You call me if you think of anything else I can pick up for you."

"Thank you." Her voice still sounded weak.

The "reds" finally got the "blues" out, thanks to Tim fielding a ground ball. Tim was standing by the bat rack. Jay walked over to him and put an arm around him. "Good fielding on that last hit."

Tim looked up at him and beamed. "Coach said it was good, too."

Jay took a deep breath. He wasn't quite sure how much to tell Tim, but he decided not to mention Becky, since that would likely get back to Emma, and just now he didn't want any more complications in any of his relationships. Plus, he didn't know how Tim would react to his leaving to do something for Becky, even though Tim had just told him that he liked her.

"Tim, I've had a call from a friend who needs me to pick up some medicine and deliver it right now. I should be back here in about half an hour or so, and I *will* be back, no matter what. I'm really sorry. Is this okay with you?"

"Sure, Dad, I'll be fine. I'm going to hit a home run today, but I'll wait 'til you get back!"

Jay smiled at Tim's humorous boast and gave him another hug. "OK. I'm going to ask Mr. Prosky to watch out for you, in case you get that home run or something—he can take a picture."

Jay walked back to the stands rapidly. Mitch Prosky was sitting on the aisle. His son played right field and was one of Tim's best friends. "Mitch, I need favor. I've got to leave practice for a little while to help out a friend who's sick. Can you watch out for Tim? I've got my cell phone with me, so call me if anything happens." Jay scribbled down the number on the back of a scrap of paper he had in his pocket.

"Sure thing, Jay! Hope your friend is going to be all right. We'll be here when you get back."

Jay climbed into the truck and started off for the Medicine Shoppe. Just as he turned the corner at the end of the first block, he felt sure he saw a sheriff's car parked a couple of blocks back to the south of the ball field.

CHAPTER THIRTY-EIGHT

IN EIGHTEEN MINUTES, Jay arrived at Becky's apartment complex with the pills and the Imodium. He noticed her car parked across the street. He hoped she had left her door unlocked in case she was confined to her bathroom or bedroom, but when he got upstairs, her door was locked. He pounded and called. If the neighbors were home and could hear him, too bad. He had a sick lady here.

He waited a couple of minutes and then knocked again. No one came. Finally, he pulled out his phone and called her. After four rings, it went to voice mail.

"This is Becky. Please leave a message, and I'll get back to you."

Feeling desperate now, he said "Becky, I'm outside your door. Please open up." Nothing. Maybe she was too weak to talk or walk? Maybe she had passed out.

He had never met any of her neighbors, but he decided to try knocking on doors. No one came out from the apartment next to hers, but across the hall, a middle-aged woman answered his knock. "Excuse me, but I'm looking for Rebecca Franz. She lives across the hall from you. I'm trying to deliver some medicine to her. Do you know if she is home?"

"Sorry, I don't. I think I saw her out by her car this morning, but I can't be sure. I had just gotten up, and I didn't have my glasses on. Is anything wrong?"

Jay tried to smile. "No, but she wanted me to deliver a prescription. I must have got her message wrong. If it's all right with you, I'm going to leave her pills and her other medicine with you. She sounded pretty much under the weather when she called me, but maybe she's feeling better. Maybe you could knock on her door later—or call her? If you see her, will you tell her that Jay was here and that she should call me?"

"Sure," the woman said, looking at him with mild interest, taking the Medicine Shoppe white bag and then closing the door.

Jay waited a minute and then knocked on Becky's door again. No response. "Should I call the sheriff?" he wondered. She might be in there and unconscious. He tried her phone again but still no answer.

He wanted to get back to Tim, realizing he had already been gone more than thirty minutes. He walked reluctantly to his truck. Just after he sped away from the first stop light, it started to rain. Jay slowed down enough that his tires would not slip on the wet pavement if he had to stop suddenly. Well, he wasn't going to see Tim hit a home run today.

By the time Jay got back to the ball field, many of the cars were gone, but he could see a few people at the field house, standing under the overhang, clear of the rain. He jumped out of the truck and ran to the small group. A quick scan told him all he needed to know—Tim was not there.

But Mitch Prosky was. He stood next to his son, talking with the coach. "Jay—you got back. We thought maybe you weren't coming."

"Where's Tim?"

"Well, I was going to give him a ride home, but a car came up right near the bleachers just after the rain started and the boys were coming off the field. Someone waved and called to Tim, and he went over to the car. He yelled back at me, 'Mr. Prosky, I've got a ride!' He had his mitt and all, so I guess he knew who it was and he got right in. Hope that was okay."

"No, no it wasn't—it is the worst thing that could have happened!" Jay wanted to scream, but he didn't. Instead, he asked, "Do you remember anything about the car? Did you get a look at the driver?"

"Not really. Some kind of dark colored sedan, I guess. Couldn't really see who was in it—just a hand waving. Tim must have known the driver, I guess. Couldn't tell if it was a man or a woman. I'm real sorry, Jay. I thought that if Tim knew the driver it was all right. Maybe it was your wife?"

Jay felt hot all over, yet his feet would not move. He had to call Emma. "Thanks, Mitch. I'm sure Tim is fine. I'll give Emma a call."

Without speaking to anyone else there, Jay turned and walked back to his truck. With the door closed, he dialed Emma.

"Em, it's me. I had to leave Tim's practice for a little while, and it started to rain. When I got back, Tim had apparently gotten a ride from one of the parents. Is he home yet?" He tried to keep his voice steady.

"No, he's not here. What do you mean by *apparently*? Don't you know who it was?" Her voice rose on this last question.

"I'm not sure. Mitch Prosky was going to take him home in case I didn't get back, but someone else picked him up. It was probably one of the other parents and they've taken the boys for something to eat. Let me sort it out. You call me when Tim gets home, or I'll call you as soon as I know something." Jay ended the call without waiting for Emma to reply.

He could not bear having to tell her that he thought their son might have been taken again.

And maybe that was not what happened. Maybe this was all a big mix up. Jay looked out of the window of the truck's cab. It was still raining but not hard. His mind went back to Becky briefly — why hadn't she called him? Then he realized that he had not seen the sheriff's car, not on his way back and not since he had been here. Where was it? Maybe one of the deputies had picked Tim up. But wouldn't Mitch have mentioned that it was a sheriff's car that Tim got into? It was time to call Sheriff Carlson. Jay dialed the number.

CHAPTER THIRTY-NINE

VIC BARTLE WAS talking to himself. It was a habit when he was angry or disturbed. *I should have done something sooner. I should have gotten Goertz out of the way sooner. I knew he was a bad actor back when we did the drug bust. No telling what the boy might eventually remember.*

He was keeping so many secrets—from Louise, from his family. And now someone was going to pay for them. Vic drove carefully. He needed to concentrate on where he was going, but he also needed to decide what to do next.

§ § §

Chris Carlson picked up Jay's call. "Jay, get over here as soon as you can. I'll get an all-points bulletin out. And I'll get a hold of Vic and get him back on duty. Don't talk to anybody else until you get here."

Chris sounded worried, which did nothing to reassure Jay. He was parking in front of the sheriff's office when his phone rang. Hoping it was Emma or Becky, he glanced at the incoming number and did not recognize it.

"Hello?"

"Jay," a familiar voice said. "It's me, Sid. How you doing? Is this a bad time?"

Jay gritted his teeth. If this was a social call, he would be civil and end it. He decided to tell Sid the truth.

"Sid, it's pretty bad. Tim is missing again. I think someone else took him. I'm at the sheriff's office. Can I call you later?"

"Damn, Jay. Sorry to hear that. But, listen, why I called you, well, it may have something to do with all that's been going on. Deb's been talking to me. She's feeling bad about everything. Today she told me she thought Mike may have had another girlfriend, I mean, even while he was seeing Deb. She doesn't know for sure. I just thought you should know that. I'm real sorry if Tim is in trouble. Anything I can do?"

Jay tried to process what Sid had just told him. Was there any connection with Tim's disappearance?

"Listen, Sid, thanks. I need to talk with the sheriff right now. Can I call you later? Or, if Deb tells you anything else, can you call me?"

"You know it, Jay. Let me know what happens and if I can help."

"Yeah, thanks Sid, I will. Thanks."

Jay was inside the sheriff's office in thirty seconds.

After Jay explained his own movements of the past two hours, he asked, "Did you have a car following Tim? I thought I saw one of your white cars following us when we went to the ball field and, later, parked down the block."

Chris Carlson consulted his laptop. "The official orders were to watch your home. Even if the deputy on duty, Armillio Sanchez, saw you take Tim in your truck, he was supposed to tail you wherever you went. He gets a short break when he needs one, but then he would have come back to the ball field, so you probably did see his car. But I don't know why he wasn't there when you came back from your friend's apartment." Jay had told Chris about Becky's call, and Chris promised to have someone go to her apartment to investigate whether she was having a medical emergency or was in some kind of trouble.

The sheriff picked up his phone and punched in a number. "Armillio, it's Chris. Did you go off the Berg surveillance this afternoon?" There was a pause while Chris listened. Then he said, "Yes, I see. No, that's all right. But I need to reach him. If he calls you for any reason, have him call me right away."

Chris turned to Jay. "Armillio *was* watching the ball field. But just after he got there, Vic drove up, parked next to him, and said he was taking over the surveillance. Armillio didn't think to check with me. He said he thought it was a little strange that Vic was driving his personal car instead of one of our squad cars, but nothing seemed wrong, so Armillio left. We'd had a report on the scanner of a fire over near the county library and so that's where he headed."

"But why wouldn't Vic have taken Tim home? And you said you were putting out an all-points bulletin. Wouldn't he have called in? What's going on here?" Jay got up and started pacing in Chris's small office.

Chris poured a glass of water for Jay and silently handed it to him. "He could've taken the scanner out of his car. I do that all the time with mine. I've already tried to call him on the police radio, but he may not have that with him, either. Tried his cell phone. My call went immediately to voice mail, so he's probably turned the phone off. But we have another option."

Jay stopped pacing and looked at the Sheriff. He wasn't processing anything very well, and he simply couldn't take in the idea that Vic Bartle had abducted Tim. "What do you mean?"

Chris leaned back in his chair, took off his glasses, and rubbed his eyes. "Two years ago, I personally attached a radio tracking tag to all the cars in our fleet and to the personal cars of Vic and all my deputies. None of them know about the personal car tags. They work. I check them every day, at least when I'm here. So, even if we can't trace the men through their cell phones, I've got the radio locater." He got up, went to a locked closet, unlocked it, and pulled out the computer and screen that were on rollers inside. "Let's see where Vic's car is now and if he's moving."

A few key strokes later, and they saw a moving object. "That's his transmitter," Chris told Jay. The car was in the western part of the county, on one of the main roads. "Can't tell where he's going to end up, but he's heading west. I'll put out a call on the police radio and then call him on his phone again."

One minute later it was clear Vic wasn't answering. "He's technically still on leave, but something's wrong." Chris concentrated on the target on the computer screen. "I'll send Armillio out after him and then ..." He turned to where Jay had been standing, but Jay was gone. The last words Jay heard before barging out the door to his truck were, "he's technically still on leave..." Jay had seen where Vic was driving—county highway 603. He was already racing the old truck above the speed limit when the sheriff got on his phone to Armillio Sanchez.

CHAPTER FORTY

"W HERE ARE WE going for our treat?" Tim asked after they had been driving for a few minutes. "I wonder why Dad hasn't called you back. I hope he can join us!"

Now came the hard part—the questions. If Tim still didn't remember anything that could be damaging, he was safe and could be taken home after all. But if he said anything, anything at all about remembering who Mike Goertz was working with, there would have to be another ending.

They were on a road that would eventually take them to the lake, to a deserted cabin there, not far from where Tim had been tied up in the boat. Plenty of ways to dispose of him there, if necessary. There was a bottle of chloroform on the floor in the back of the car to subdue him, if it came to that, and ropes in the trunk, along with a shovel. The license plates on the car, which was borrowed for the day from a friend, had been switched with the real ones and would tie back to an abandoned truck in the next county. Also, there was mud all over the brown car, so even the color was hard to identify. *Always plan ahead*. Good motto, although Mike Goertz hadn't paid as much attention to it as he should have.

Time to check the rear view mirror. It looked like there had been a car following them earlier, but there wasn't anything suspicious now. Only a few more minutes and this would all be over.

"Tim, I worry a lot about everything that happened to you—and to Colley. Your dad told me it was bad for you. Did Mike Goertz, that man who kidnapped you, ever say anything about somebody else helping him? Did you hear him talking to anybody else? Because if he did, that person might be trying to find you."

Tim shook his head. "No, I don't remember." He'd told all this to the police before, but he thought hard. He hoped he wasn't in any more trouble just when everything seemed to be fine. Then he did remember something.

"When I was in that basement and I made up the story about Dad having money for the ransom, I had to give him Dad's cell phone number. He was going to write a text to Dad, and I looked to be sure he put Dad's number in his phone right. I saw a couple of the numbers he already had in his phone, and I remember them. I'm good at remembering things with numbers. Do you think that matters? I haven't told anyone 'cause I just thought of it now when you asked."

"What were the numbers?"

Tim recited them, hoping he remembered correctly. "Maybe if I think hard, I can remember if there was a name or, like, a picture with them."

The driver sighed. "Well, it's smart of you to remember. That could help. Since we haven't heard from your dad yet, we're going to take a little side trip to do something before we have out treat. And I need to get something out of the back seat right now. Then we'll try your dad again, okay?"

Tim nodded.

CHAPTER FORTY-ONE

J ay could see Vic's silver Nissan now, about a quarter mile ahead. The county road was curvy, and it wasn't easy to keep the car in sight, but the traffic was light this time of day. Jay sped up. He didn't know what he was going to do when he caught up with Vic, but right now he was concentrating on stopping him. It looked like there was another car, a brown sedan further ahead of Vic, but Jay wasn't interested in that vehicle—only what he needed to do with Vic.

Suddenly, the brown car made a sharp right turn. Vic's Nissan braked abruptly. Jay, who was speeding and following Vic closely, rear-ended Vic's car hard. Jay thought he could see Vic's head hit the windshield.

Jay jumped out of the truck. He wasn't hurt. He wished now that he had a gun. He got to the driver's side window and saw Vic slumped over the wheel. Jay tore open the door and tried to push Vic upright. "Where's Tim? Where's my son?" Without realizing it, he was shaking Vic, who didn't respond.

Jay looked frantically through the Nissan. He could see everything inside the car—no Tim. He went to the back and realized the trunk was locked. He ran back to Vic, who was just now trying to sit up. Jay started to yell, "OPEN THE TRUNK. I WANT MY BOY."

Vic looked at him groggily for a second. Then his eyes cleared. "I don't have him, Jay. She's got him." He point down the winding, rutted road, but there was nothing Jay could see. Jay had his hands on Vic's throat. Even though Vic was the larger man, Jay's anger was fueling his strength.

"Becky's got him, Jay. Becky. She's going to the lake. Get me into your truck!"

For a full two seconds, Jay stood still. His hands dropped from Vic's neck. He simply could not understand what he had just heard. "*Becky* has Tim? *Becky*?"

Vic was out of his car, pulling Jay toward the truck. "We have to go after them. NOW." He heaved himself up into the truck's passenger seat and watched while Jay fumbled for his keys. Vic pulled a phone out of his pocket and made the call he should have made hours ago. "Chris, it's me, Vic, we're at the lake on Harts' road. Get someone up here. Tim's been kidnapped, and we're tailing the kidnapper."

Jay started up, drove around the Nissan, and sped down what was little more than a gravel path. In his side mirror, he saw flashing lights out on the county road behind him. He hoped this meant help. He saw the brown car slowing down way ahead. A figure got out and opened the door on the passenger's side.

Jay suddenly realized that Vic was slumped over in the passenger seat. Jay reached over to shake him. No response. "Oh god, he's fainted or something," Jay realized. Vic's gun was on his hip. Jay screeched to a stop and, with some difficulty, pulled the pistol free, taking the safety off as quickly as he could. He started up again. Now the figure from the brown car had a bundle from the front seat awkwardly balanced and was trying to lift it. Jay stopped the truck and leaped out.

"Becky! Stop! It's me. Let me have Tim. It's okay, it's okay. Let me have Tim." He was running toward her as fast as he had ever run, and somehow he was pointing the pistol. She turned and stopped lifting for a moment, letting Jay gain a few more feet. Then she turned back toward the car and started shoving the bundle back inside.

Jay knelt and took aim. A second after the blanketed bundle was almost out of sight in the car, Jay fired. Her left arm dropped. Another shot rang out, and Jay, still in his crouch, turned. A few feet behind him and to his left was Deputy Sheriff Armillio Sanchez, who had just put a bullet into Becky's stomach, and coming up fast behind both of them was Sheriff Carlson's white official car.

"Armillio, cover him and get the child!" Chris Carlson shouted, pulling out his own pistol. Jay got up and ran, with Deputy Sanchez at his side.

They got to Becky and saw she was conscious but bleeding badly and moaning, holding her right arm over the wound in her stomach. Jay looked at her for a second and then grabbed the blanketed figure out of the front seat. He gently pulled it a few feet away and pried off the blanket. Tim lay still. He looked unharmed, and Jay checked to make sure he was breathing. He was dimly aware that Armillio was handcuffing Becky.

Chris Carlson was now kneeling down on the other side of Tim. "I've called for two ambulances. We'll give Tim oxygen right away. I have it in my car. He'll be all right, Jay."

Jay couldn't speak. He gathered Tim into his arms and cradled him. "You stay with him here, and I'll get the oxygen. Armillio will take care of her." Chris Carlson ran back to his car and drove it up to Jay and Tim. He gently placed the oxygen mask over Tim's mouth and began administering it. Within seconds, Tim's eyes opened, first showing confusion and then recognition of Jay. "Try to get him to sit up," Chris advised, and Jay was able to pull Tim into a sitting position. His body felt so light.

Just then, Jay remembered that Vic was still in his truck, probably still unconscious. "Vic's back there, in my truck. I rammed him out on the highway when I thought he had Tim. He got in the truck and seemed all right, but then he passed out."

"I'll check on him," Chris said, turning to run back to Jay's truck. In another minute he was moving his car parallel to it and had the oxygen out again to work on Vic.

The ambulances came within minutes. First, they loaded Tim onto a stretcher. Jay asked permission to ride with his son. Then, they put Vic, who was conscious now but complaining of pain, on the second stretcher in the same ambulance. As they were moving Vic, Jay saw that Becky was being lifted into the second ambulance. He badly wanted to say something to her, to confront her, but there was no time.

"I'll follow all of you to the hospital," Chris Carlson said, placing a hand on Jay's shoulder. "Armillio is coming with us, too. I'll get a wrecker out here to move Vic's car and someone to drive your truck to my office. We can get her car later—I'll need to impound it."

Jay got in the back of the ambulance. The attendant was checking on Tim and offering Vic some water. Jay put a hand out to Vic and tentatively squeezed his left hand. "Sorry about your car," he said. Vic looked at him steadily. "And you saved Tim's life. I can never thank you enough for that."

"I think you had something to do with it, too," Vic answered, "and with this goddamn headache." He winced but smiled slightly and closed his eyes. Jay stared at him. He had a feeling there was a lot to talk about. He looked out the small back window of the ambulance. The rain had stopped. He suddenly realized that Carlos' truck was going to need some repairs. Well, he could deal with that later. Right now, he had his son back, and his son was going to be all right.

CHAPTER FORTY-TWO

"**V**IC WANTS TO see you." Emma came into Tim's room and gave Jay a quick kiss on the top of his head. He was holding Tim's hand, while Tim was napping. A large, unfinished Coke sat on his bed tray. Louise was in the lobby of Western General Hospital with Lynn. They were all taking turns visiting Tim and Vic. It was late, but Lynn was being allowed to stay up, and she had talked Louise into buying both of them ice cream in the coffee shop.

Jay gently released Tim's hand. "His breathing's good. The nurse said she'd be back in an hour to check on him. Maybe we can even take him home later tonight."

Emma sat down by the bed. Jay made his way to Vic's private room. The door was open. A Braves game was on the television, and Vic's bed was cranked into an upright position. A cold pack lay on a towel on the bedside table, next to a pitcher of ice water.

Vic turned when Jay came in and muted the TV's sound. "Emma tells me Tim seems fine."

Jay smiled and nodded. Vice motioned him to the chair facing the bed. "That's good. Don't know how much chloroform she gave him, but I'm glad we got him when we did." Jay noticed the "we."

"I gotta ask you something and then tell you some things." Vic paused and looked steadily at Jay. "Why did you think I had Tim?"

Jay knew he needed to be candid. "Because when I couldn't find Tim at the ball field, I went to Chris. He called Armillio, who said you told him he could leave the surveillance—that you would take over. If you had offered Tim a ride, he would've taken it. You were the only one I could think of who would do that. And there were some times in the last week I didn't know what you were up to." Jay stopped and swallowed. "I was so worried, I didn't know but that you might have gotten mixed up with Mike Goertz."

Vic grunted and winced as he moved his head slightly and reached for the cold pack. "Damn pain pills don't last long enough." There was a pause while neither man spoke. "Well, I said I had some things to tell you. Some of this Emma doesn't know, and some Louise doesn't either."

149

Jay waited.

"Five years ago, we had this drug bust. I know you've heard about it. Everybody has. I got lots of credit for breaking up the ring and getting those boys in jail. But the thing is, I didn't get all of them, and I knew it. And the one I knew about but couldn't get my hands on—or any real proof about—was Mike Goertz." Vic used his free hand to drink from his water glass.

"He'd already had some minor scrapes, and so I began keeping tabs on him when I could. I found out a lot about where he worked, although he never kept a job for long, and I usually knew who he was seeing. But I couldn't find him doing anything bad for a long time. So I more or less stopped following him. Then, last winter, he was hauled in for a DUI. The arresting deputy didn't do the breathalyzer test right, so they just charged him with speeding. He pleaded no contest and got off with a fine. I decided to check up on him again once in a while. First thing I discovered in the spring was that he seemed to have two girlfriends he was seeing fairly regularly. He wasn't a bad looking guy, so that didn't strike me as unusual."

Vic winced as he put the ice pack down. Jay began to feel very badly about having hit Vic's car so hard.

"When you came in talking about some mysterious hand in a window, I didn't connect it with anything—just thought you were imagining things, maybe hitting the bottle. I cruised by that house a few times myself, didn't see anything, didn't assign anybody, and I let it go. Remember I asked you if you had told anybody else? I didn't plan on doing anything other than a drive-by myself, but I wasn't going to tell you that." Vic looked steadily at Jay for a moment. Jay merely nodded.

"So then when you had the accident and said Tim and another boy went missing, I realized that there must have been something going on at that house, but I still didn't connect it with Goertz. I kept following him when I could, and I noticed something. The one girlfriend he was seeing had a little boy when I first started following him—at least, I figured it was her boy, 'cause he used to run out of her house. Then I didn't see the boy anymore. Didn't think much about it—kid could be sick or liked to play inside. Then you called me and told me your friend, Sid Hartman, had lost his little boy, Colley, and I knew then, even before you told me, that Mike Goertz had to be involved, because the one girlfriend he was seeing was Deborah Hartman. And the other one was Becky Franz."

"Vic, I need to ask you something."

"I'm not done yet, but shoot."

"The night of my accident, nobody could reach you. Emma tried you at home and on your cell. You came by my hospital room and said you and Louise had been out. I figured you turned your phone off so the two of you could have some fun. But later, Louise said something about not having been out with you for two months. Where were you that night?"

There was a pause, and Vic looked up at the TV and then back at Jay. "I have cancer. It's in my stomach. Found out about it three months ago. I haven't told anybody until now, not even Louise. I don't trust a lot of doctors, so I've been going to one of these homeopathic guys up in the next county. He sees me evenings twice a week. Haven't been feeling too bad lately, so what he's giving me may be helping. I went up to his clinic that night. I had the phone off."

"Vic, I'm real sorry." Jay thought that sounded lame, but he couldn't think of anything else.

"Well, don't be. I'm dealing with it. So we'll see how this goes. Anyway, when you told me it was probably Goertz who was the kidnapper, I knew I had to act. Felt it was my fault that I hadn't gotten him on drug charges five years ago or figured out the kidnapping of Sid's boy. So I wanted to be the one to capture Goertz. I was the one punctured his tires so he couldn't get away, no matter what. And I didn't order anybody else to come to the pumping station—I wanted to be the big hero, so I went there alone, planted the money, started up my car, and drove it away a few feet so he'd hear a car leaving. Then I got out to watch for him. I had two other deputies out looking for Tim, but I didn't figure there would be a shootout when Goertz picked up the money. I knew he couldn't go anywhere with flat tires, so I let him take the money and then I yelled 'stop'. I lied to you about my gun jamming; I just thought I'd grab him in his car. When he drew his gun on me, I fired to wound him, not kill him, but I guess I'm just a bad shot."

Vic managed a crooked smile. "And then when you came up, you had Becky with you. You remember when you both saw I had shot him, she stumbled off to the side and got sick? I got to thinking that maybe he hadn't been doing all what he'd been doing alone, or at least not just with Deborah Hartman. Maybe Becky knew about all of it and was even his accomplice. And I was pretty sure she didn't tell you she was dating him."

"No, she didn't. She told me she had a boyfriend, Ben, in the army. She did a lot of texting and sometimes talking on her cell, but I figured it was to Ben. Except I got a hold of her cell phone a couple of days ago and found some of the numbers she sent texts to. Looked like the main one was for her mother or someone in South Carolina. I knew Ben wasn't supposed to be from South Carolina. He'd lived in Florida, then here, and now he was supposed to be in Fort Hood in Texas. All the other numbers I saw were local. So, now I don't even know if Ben exists."

"We can check out her phone later. Might tell us a lot." Vic took another drink of water. Jay refilled his glass.

"Anyway, after I got Goertz, I tried to figure out a way to see if he had an accomplice. It certainly didn't seem like Colley's mother, Deb Hartman, really would have gone along with the kidnapping—at least not the way Goertz was keeping Colley in that house. And she wouldn't have known about Tim. So, I wondered about Becky. But maybe she didn't know anything either? The more I thought about it, the more it seemed someone had to have been helping Goertz, so I began tailing Becky. Today, I was really just watching out for Tim since I didn't have anything better to do, being 'on leave' and all." Vic's bitterness came through his voice.

"But then I saw this car come up to the ball field. It wasn't her car, at least not the one that I've seen her driving. I couldn't see who was driving, but when Tim got in, I knew I had to follow them—even if it was nothing. And I didn't know where you were. When I got close enough to take a look at the car from the back, I was pretty sure the driver was Becky. I couldn't see anybody in the passenger seat, but I figured Tim isn't tall and maybe his head just wasn't showing. I had a bad feeling, though, when they weren't driving to your house—I mean Emma's. I called in the license plate number and got the information that it used to belong to some guy in the next county who had a Chevy truck, but the plate was no longer registered. She must've borrowed or stolen a car and put the old plate on it. Anyway, then I turned off my phones so I wouldn't have to take any calls. Didn't want anyone telling me what I should be doing, you know?"

Vic paused and then actually smiled. "Guess I didn't think Chris could find me. He must've stuck a radio tracker on my car—so that's probably how you found me. Right?"

Jay nodded and thought of another question. "You think she was just going along with me when I was watching the house and all, so she could tell Goertz what I was doing?"

Vic gave Jay a hard stare. "Could be. Or could be she really liked you, and maybe, in the end, she didn't go along with all that Goertz was doing. But she must have gotten scared that Tim would remember something. You say she texted and talked a lot, so maybe Goertz talked to her sometime when Tim was listening. I don't know. But something spooked her. So she probably figured that she had to find Tim and talk to him. Maybe she would have let him go, but he must have remembered something and told her what it was."

Jay got up and went to look out the window, even though it was dark. The TV hummed in the background. Jay turned back to Vic. "I don't know what came first—her agreeing to go to the house where Colley was so she could tell Goertz that I was watching it, or maybe her even getting the road job so she could watch the house. She seemed to like Tim. She helped me find him. I don't understand how she could try to kill him."

"People do bad things when they're scared. They don't think things through. I've seen it a lot. Don't be too hard on yourself. You didn't know she had any connection with Goertz. Wish I had figured it out sooner."

"Can I talk to her, ask her some questions?" Jay turned back toward the chair and sat down.

"Maybe. But not tonight. Why don't you go back to Emma and Tim and see if they'll let him go home? Let me know if you all leave. I'll do some checking and call you in the morning. Doc has already told me they're going to keep me here for observation even though I have a pretty thick head." Jay didn't know if this last was meant as a joke, but he smiled.

"Thanks, Vic. For everything. It's going to be hard explaining to Tim why this lady he liked tried to hurt him, but maybe I can tell him some way that he can understand. If he comes out of all this without being frightened of people, I'll feel like we've won a prize or something."

"Oh, yeah, one more thing. I've already talked with Chris. In the official report on what happened today, it'll say I shot Becky in the arm, not you, and Armillio put the bullet in her stomach. It was my gun you used. So, anyway, you won't be going through any hearing or anything."

Jay thanked him again and left. When he got back to Tim's room, he found his son dressed and sitting on the side of the bed. Emma had her arm around him, and they were both smiling. "Dad! The doctor said I can go now!" Tim reached up to hug his father.

Jay turned questioningly to Emma. "Yes, they've checked everything. His breathing and heart rate are fine. So we can go home."

There was a pause while Emma and Tim both looked at Jay. Without hesitation, he said, "And I'm going there with you."

"Good, let's pick up Lynn in the lobby and tell Louise she's free to go. She probably wants to spend some time with Vic." Emma's smile broadened.

And right then she gave Jay a quick kiss on the cheek. It felt like the second best thing that had happened to him all day.

CHAPTER FORTY-THREE

S HE COULDN'T GET out of the leg restraints on the bed, and there was a deputy outside her hospital door, but the floor nurse was acting nice enough to her. Becky's left shoulder and upper arm were heavily bandaged, but she raised her right arm and rang the call button.

"Can I get you something?" The young Indonesian nurse asked.

"I need to write something down. Can you get me a pen or pencil and some paper?"

"I'll be back in a minute." The nurse consulted her instructions. This patient was not allowed to have some things, such as scissors or anything else sharp—not even a hair comb. But a soft-tipped pen and paper were not on the forbidden list.

With the tablet and pen on top of the bed table, Becky awkwardly raised herself up and began to write. When she finished, she folded the paper over twice and wrote "Jay Berg" on the outside. Then she rang the call button for the nurse again.

"Here. Please take this. You can give it to the sheriff or one of his men when they come to your desk. They'll come."

The nurse hesitated for a moment, took the folded note, and left.

Becky lay back. Jay would probably not believe her, but she hoped he would at least read the note. The funny thing was—if anything about all this could be considered funny—she had really begun to care for him. If only she could have been sure what Tim did or didn't know about her, she might have found a better solution than getting rid of him. She didn't like children, but she didn't mind this one. He was brave. But he had seen her cell phone number on Mike's phone and might remember seeing her name, too. It had been a stroke of luck when Mike's phone had been found that all messages and entries were apparently erased, or she would have been questioned by the police earlier. Tim's memory of seeing her number on that phone meant her luck had run out. She had worked too hard for too long to let a ten-year-old kid ruin her life.

After she realized that the second boy Mike kidnapped was Tim, she had warned Mike that Tim's father had no money. As usual, Mike was stubborn. "You don't know shit about it. Kid said the money is a secret. We're gonna get something out of this mess. I'll take care of that. No one needs to get hurt. You just keep the father on track."

She knew the money drop was going to be some kind of a trap. At least, she was lucky enough later to find Colley walking down that road and get him home without anyone knowing who she was. She wondered sometimes, now especially, about why she had hooked up with Mike in the first place. But she knew: his looks, his ambition, his schemes that sounded good at first, his willingness to talk about a future together with lots of money. He was the most exciting man she had ever met, and he paid a lot of attention to her. The sex was better than good. And there would be real money. That always mattered to her.

After the kidnapping of Tim, all she hoped was that Mike would escape, Tim would be found, and the whole thing would just blow over. *Fat chance.* She had thought she might decide to break up with Mike after that and see where things led with Jay. There was no "Ben", of course, and never had been, but "Ben" was a convenient excuse for her to cover the texting and occasional phone calls with Mike. Later, it got more complicated, when she began to like Jay. She wondered how much he had already figured out. Did he know that once he showed her the house where Mike was keeping Colley that she had told Mike that the hiding place was no longer safe? If only Mike hadn't been careless with his cigarettes, there wouldn't have been the fire and Jay wouldn't have gotten Colley.

She knew Jay would try to find her, to see her. That was why she had written the note, telling him almost everything. She didn't plan to be there when he came.

The pain in her stomach was returning. Becky started to moan. Softly at first, then louder. She began to make gasping sounds. Finally, the door opened, and the young deputy guarding her room hesitantly took a few steps in.

"Please, I need water!" She motioned toward the dresser a few feet from the bed. The deputy looked around, saw the water pitcher and a glass, poured some water, and brought it to her, setting it on her bed tray. "Help me sit up," she said in a whisper. He bent down to find the crank on the side of her bed.

Even though her left shoulder and arm hurt like crazy, she could move. She turned, picked up the large paper cup full of water with her right hand, and threw it at his head. He flinched and reached with both hands to clear his eyes, giving her just enough time to snap open his gun holster and yank out his pistol. Holding it in her right hand, she painfully took off the safety with her left.

"Now, I'm already going down for kidnapping a little boy, so I don't mind shooting you. Get the cuffs off my legs. Hurry."

The young deputy was so stunned he could barely move, but he realized this woman was serious. He could see the call bell but knew that if he tried to reach for it, she really might pull the trigger. Better to get the leg restraints off and then wrestle her to the ground before she tried to shoot. He took out the keys to the cuffs. Working as fast as he could, he got them both off within a minute.

"Now, get in that closet and count to ten before you come out." She was going to get out. She could climb through her window and make it to the ground. It was a first floor room. After that, she would have to find a house to break into and find some clothes. She hadn't thought much beyond that, but she knew she had to get away from the hospital.

The deputy turned toward the closet door as if to open it. Then he whirled around again and started back for her. The loud clang startled them both. It came from just inside the door. Becky jerked her head around, and in that second the deputy went for her legs. Becky turned back to him, but Vic hit her gun arm hard, and she dropped the gun. Feeling him twist her arm back, she screamed, but they had her pinned now. The bed pan, doubling as Vic's weapon, lay in a corner.

"Get the cuffs back on her feet!" Vic yelled.

He took off his belt and secured Becky's arms in front of her. Then he picked up the deputy's gun and handed it back to him. "Get another set of cuffs. You got some in your car?" The young deputy looked dazed but nodded and hurried out.

"Sweetheart, you're not goin' anywhere!" Vic turned as the Indonesian nurse came hurrying into the room.

"Is anything wrong?" She looked at the restraints on Becky. She saw the bed pan on the floor and picked it up, replacing it on the rolling cart near the door.

"No, not now. We need to keep this one more quiet," Vic replied, jerking his head toward Becky, who so far had not said a word. The nurse looked at Becky and at Vic and then decided to leave the room. She would be doing her rounds later and could be sure the patient was all right. This wasn't the first prisoner she had nursed on her floor, but it always made her nervous.

When the deputy came back with the cuffs, Vic attached one to Becky's left wrist and then to the iron siding of the bed. He looked at her. "I'm going to leave you a hand free to call the nurse, but if we have any more trouble with you, that cuff goes on, too." The deputy went back outside the room to his chair.

Vic looked at Becky for several minutes. She would not meet his gaze. Finally, he said, "You ever gonna tell Jay what you were up to?"

Finally, she looked at him. "Bastard!"

Vic smiled. "Yeah, that's me. Probably much worse than your old boyfriend. I've been after him for years, but I didn't figure him for a kidnapper. Plus he would have gladly shot me out at the pumping station. Maybe we could have got him for attempted murder, too, if he lived. That's probably what they'll charge you with."

Becky looked away again. In a much lower voice she said, "There's a letter for Jay I left with the nurse. I'd like him to get it."

Vic looked at her for a few more seconds. "Okay," he said finally. Then, "I'm leaving you now. We're keeping you in here until you can stand to go to jail. Any more games and you'll go there right away, regardless." He knew this wasn't strictly true, as they had no medical facilities at the jail, but he wanted to put the fear of God into her.

Becky turned her face away from Vic and did not answer.

§§§

On the way back to his room, Vic stopped by the nurse's station. "Patient in 109 says she left a letter for a Jay Berg. I'll take that and see that he gets it." Vic was wearing his uniform shirt and pants, with his belt now replaced, but no gun holster. He had left that in his room, but the bed pan had served the purpose.

The young nurse gave him the letter. "Shall I check on her now? Is she all right?"

"You can check. We've had to add a hand cuff, but she can still use the call bell. She'll probably be here for a couple of days—doc will have to decide that."

Vic took the letter and walked back to his room one floor up. The nurse on his floor was making the rounds. "If you can, give me an extra dose of something for my head," he asked her when she came to his room. "Hurts like hell."

She was surprised to see him out of bed and in uniform, but after he put his hospital gown back on, she took his temperature, fluffed his pillows, filled his water pitcher, and handed him a small cup with four red pills in it. "If these don't work, let me know and I'll see if we can get you something stronger."

Vic grunted. All he wanted now was a good night's sleep.

He placed the folded letter inside his jacket pocket. He was curious, but no way was he going to read Jay's private mail.

Chapter Forty-Four

EMMA AND JAY finally got Tim and Lynn to bed, although it was very late. Lynn was having a pleasant sugar high and wanted more ice cream, which they refused her. She finally fell asleep, clutching her stuffed elephant. Tim was quiet but wanted to hold Jay's hand for a long time, and Jay let him. In the time they were alone, Jay did his best to explain to Tim about Becky.

"She was frightened, Tim. She made some bad choices. Mike Goertz had been her boyfriend. She was probably in on the kidnapping of Colley. But she liked you, and I don't think she really wanted to hurt you. People do bad things sometimes when they are scared. She won't hurt you now — she'll be going away to prison for a long time."

Tim looked at his father without saying anything, and finally nodded. Then he reached over to hug Jay. "Thanks, Dad, for rescuing me. You and Uncle Vic." His eye lids dropped a couple of times, and he didn't say anything more. Finally, when Jay heard Tim's slow, rhythmic breathing, he tiptoed out of the room.

"He's asleep," he told Emma, who was fixing hot tea for both of them. They sat down at the kitchen table to drink it. "I can stay tonight, but I have to go back and get some clothes and get to work in the morning, if that's all right." After they left the hospital, Emma had driven him to the Sheriff's office where Jay picked up Carlos' truck from the parking lot. The front end looked terrible, but at least it ran.

Emma closed her eyes briefly and then looked at Jay. "It's all right for you to go. I can always take a nap tomorrow if Tim keeps me up tonight, but I think they both may sleep through."

They sipped their tea. "Emma, we have a lot to talk about — if you'd like to. Maybe not right now, but soon."

Emma nodded. "Yes, I know. We've been going in different directions. Maybe we can talk about that."

Jay found the next words more difficult. "I just want you to know nothing much really happened with Becky. And I never knew she was involved with Mike Goertz."

Emma reached out to squeeze his left hand. "I know. And you had every right to be seeing someone. I was." She paused and then added, "Patrick and I have broken up."

"Oh?" Jay meant it as more of a question than a comment.

"He's a good man, but I told him I wasn't sure about you and me."

Jay felt his face flush. Were they going to have this conversation now? But he had to go on now. He reached for her hand. "You told me a few months ago that you 'didn't want to live like this anymore.' I never really knew what you meant."

"Well, you were working so hard and always trying to get a second job. And for a while, you were hitting the beer pretty hard. You were good with Tim and Lynn, but I just felt like you didn't care about me anymore."

Jay sighed. It was true, and yet it wasn't. "I'm sorry about the drinking—I'm being pretty careful about that now, and I guess it was just to get over feeling that things weren't right with us. But I do worry about money, and I need a better job than what I have now. I don't like it that you bring in more than I do."

Emma looked at him steadily. "But I don't mind that. You'll find something else. I just wanted to do things together like we used to. Maybe go to a movie, or have a picnic. Just us. I've missed that."

Jay wanted to tell her how much he missed her and the family. He wanted to tell her he didn't like living alone, that Becky was someone who filled a hole in his life. But he couldn't quite find the words, so all he said was, "I'd like to move back in. If that works for you. I'd like us to try again."

Emma got up from her chair, came around behind Jay and hugged him hard. "I'd like that very much, and so would Lynn and Tim. Very much."

For the first time in two weeks Jay felt a profound sense of relief. He held both of Emma's hands in his for a moment and then got up. "Look, I better get back to the apartment. I do have to go to work in the morning. After work, I'll pick up most of my clothes and come back here—if that's okay with you. I can move the rest of the stuff out next weekend."

Emma touched his cheek. "That will be fine. I'll cook dinner. And the adults can have a glass of wine. I think we deserve it."

Jay hugged her again and said, "Let me check on Tim one more time."

They both went upstairs and looked in on the sleeping boy. His baseball mitt lay on the floor near the head of his bed. His breathing was deep and steady. "I think miracles sometimes happen," Jay whispered to Emma. They left Tim's room together.

CHAPTER FORTY-FIVE

J ay got the call on his cell phone early in the morning, while he was driving to work.

"Jay, it's me, Vic. They're springing me from the hospital this morning, and I have something to deliver to you. Can I drop by your work site around lunch time? When do you get off?"

"That's fine, Vic. My break comes at 11:30. How're you feeling?"

"Much better than I was right after you rammed me!"

He'll never let me forget that, Jay thought, resigned to a lifetime of being teased.

When he arrived at the job site, Carlos looked horrified when he saw his truck. "Jay, what hit you?"

"Carlos, I'm sorry. It's more like I hit something, but I'll pay for the damage." Jay hesitated. He felt he owed Carlos some explanation, so he gave him a short version of the story. The hard part was talking about Becky. "She won't be coming back, Carlos, at least not today and probably not at all. I'm sorry."

If Carlos was shocked, he didn't show it. He put an arm around Jay's shoulder. "The truck's insured, so if the sheriff will back you up, I'll just file a claim for an accident. I am very sorry you and your family have had so much trouble, and I am glad you have your boy back, safe and sound."

The day proved to be the hottest yet. The previous day's rain only cooled things off briefly. Now, the road was steamy. Jay felt exhausted after his first hour of work. Promptly at 11:30, Vic pulled up in his car. He saw Jay under the pine trees and walked over to join him. As he squatted down, he pulled out a folded paper from his pocket and handed it to Jay.

"Becky wrote a note to you. I told the hospital I would deliver it."

Jay took the paper but did not open it. "Did you see her? Talk to her? How is she?"

Vic squatted down next to Jay. "Physically she's all right, but she's in even more trouble." He related the events of the night before.

All Jay could say was, "Wow!" And then almost to himself, "I would never have guessed she could turn violent."

Vic coughed. "People do strange things when they are fighting for their lives, or at least their freedom. If she'd escaped, I don't think she would've come after Tim again or tried to harm you, but you never know."

Jay unfolded the paper and began to read it to himself. After he was finished, he was silent for a few minutes. He suspected that Vic wanted to know what she wrote.

"It's pretty much like you thought. She says she was involved with Mike Goertz, that she knew he had taken Colley and hidden him. Becky found a vacant house that was on the market and she even removed the original 'for sale' sign so no one could call about the house as long as they stored College there. Goertz told Deb Hartman that he would keep the boy in a safe place where some people would take good care of him. Goertz thought he could get a ransom because Sid Hartman was coming into money. When she met me and found out I knew about the house and saw Colley, she kept an eye on me and warned Goertz." Jay paused. "Then, she claims she told him not to keep Tim after the accident, but he did because Tim told him I had money." This next was harder, but Jay kept going. "And she says she began to care about me."

"Strange way to show that, trying to kill your son!" Vic raised his voice more than he meant to.

"She asks me to forgive her. That she is going away and will never show up here again."

"Yeah, she's going away all right. You can count on that." Vic thought of something. "You still want to see her? She'll probably be in the hospital for a couple more days, under guard, of course."

Jay had thought about just that question. Earlier yesterday, he would have said he did. Now, looking again at the letter, he said quietly, "No, I don't think so. She may not have answered all my questions, but there's no point." He could not explain to Vic that he did still care what happened to her, that he did not regret the few good moments they had, that he deeply regretted what she had done. But it was over with Becky, finished.

The two men fell silent. Jay thought he could see kindness in Vic's eyes. Finally, Vic said, "Well, guess I'll be going. Looks like I'm going to be back on duty by Saturday. State Police have cleared me for the Goertz shooting, and Chris say's there's not even going to an inquiry about Armillio and me shooting Becky." He actually winked at Jay, who grimaced and simply said, "Thanks."

Jay got up to walk Vic to his car. On the way, he said, "Vic, I'm moving back into my house over the next couple of days. Maybe you and Louise could come over for dinner one night? I know Tim would like to see you. Can Emma give you a call?"

Vic beamed at Jay. "You bet! I'm going to share the cancer thing with Lou when I see her tonight. I'll tell Emma, too. And I'm telling Chris. There've been too many secrets."

Jay reached out to shake his brother-in-law's hand. They might never become best friends, but he thought they might learn to respect each other and maybe even go beyond that.

After work, Jay went to his apartment to clean up and pack clothes. He called Alex Rosen and left a message on Alex's voice mail that he would not be renewing the apartment lease. He added that he could help Alex in the orchard during the coming weekend. Maybe there was still a chance to get a job with Alex, working toward part ownership of the orchard. He would feel Alex out about that on Saturday. He meant to call Sid, too, and fill him in on all the developments, but the day went by too fast. Jay decided to call him tomorrow.

Before he left to drive over to his house, he pulled out Becky's letter again. He reread her last sentences.

"Please don't hate me. I think you are a good man, and I could have loved you. I hope you can go back to your family. I was not the right person for you, but I will think of you always."

Not the right person. Yes, that's true, Jay thought. He had made some poor choices in the past, but he was going to try to be the right person for his family. It might not be easy—he and Emma both had some baggage, but he was going to try as hard as he could.

He carried his suitcase to the car and came back to lock the apartment door. The heat was dissipating, and the sun slanted across the apple orchard, giving the apples a golden sheen. On impulse, he ran into the orchard and picked four ripe apples. *One for each of us.* He did not want to arrive on his own doorstep tonight without presents. But he knew that, for him, having the four of them together again would be the best present of all.

ALSO BY ELIZABETH YOUNG

Fugo: Terror From the Sky

In November, 1944, the Japanese began launching 9,300 unmanned bomb-carrying balloons (Fugo) that were carried east over the Pacific Ocean by the jet stream. Now, almost 70 years later, a group of terrorists using modern technology will try and succeed where the Japanese failed. It will be up to an unlikely group to find a way to stop one of the deadliest terrorist attacks on US soil.

Do You See Him Now
(May 2011, Infinity Publishing)

Ellie Courtland has been haunted for thirty-three years, having witnessed the murder of her mother, an FBI agent. She has always hoped to remember more about the murderer. Suddenly, she sees a picture that looks like him. She teams with the FBI to identify him. But he is looking for her, too, and her search tips him off. Everyone is a suspect—her mother's former partner, a friend's father, even her own long estranged father. While Ellie juggles the two men in her life, her teaching and her search, the murderer is closing in.

The Seven Sorrows
by Gregg Kuehn

A set of still-lethal handheld tactical nuclear weapons, stolen from the United States Army during the Cold War, has been hidden deep in a cave on the island of El Fortunato, British West Indies, since the Cuban Missile Crisis. KC Jameson finds himself in a race to retrieve the weapons. Can KC decipher the one clue to the missles whereabouts before they fall into the wrong hands? And exactly whose hands are the wrong hands?

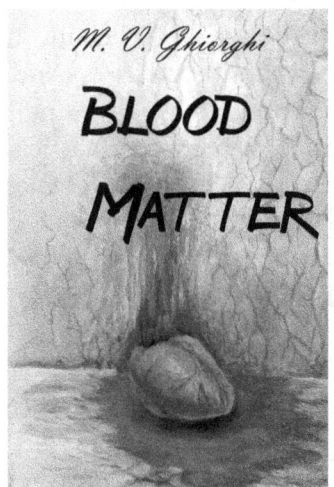

Blood Matters
by M.V. Ghiorghi

A broken-hearted FBI Agent on the run from his demons…a sadistic genius with a penchant for vengeance…a beautiful forensic psychiatrist with a monstrous past…A doomed love triangle born of crime. Can Agent Vasquez survive the *Blood Matter*?

A Bother of Bodies
by A.J. Capper

Mabel Fuller and her brother are on the run because of Mabel's attempt to kill their mother fifteen years ago. But they're not worried about the law. Their main concern is the family that raised them, the McAllisters. Mabel and Dean manage to avoid the large Irish network with frequent moves and aliases. Or, so they thought. When dead bodies turn up in Dean's newly-purchased barn, the brother and sister fear the McAllisters have found them. Until they realize it's something worse...

The 8th Doll
by Chris Rakunas

When the body of geologist Charlie Landry is found beheaded beside the cenote at Dzibilchaltun, Skips Kane calls his old friend Professor Alex Guidry. Their only clue turns out to be a small doll with the number "8" written in Charlie's own blood. The mystery of the 8th doll will take Kane and Guidry down the winding paths of the Yucatan where they will discover the answer to the age old question: what will happen when the Mayan calendar ends?